"Don't you ever stop talking?" Ryan asked huskily.

Maggie would've been offended if his eyes hadn't been sparkling like the clearest seawaters beneath his long black lashes, if his lips hadn't been quirked suggestively. He wanted to kiss her. And she wanted him to, she realized with a knot of excitement.

But why? He was right, she never did stop talking—or thinking or questioning, for that matter. This mutual attraction was probably just natural curiosity.

She felt herself being pulled closer and closer to Ryan, with a dizzy anticipation. Amazingly, she couldn't feel his touch anywhere. It was as though she was being drawn by a magnetic force.

Maggie lowered her eyes to find both of his hands still cradling the baby. It was Annabella who was playing cupid! With a handful of Maggie's hair for a tow rope, she was tugging her on a steady course toward Ryan.

The moment his mouth covered hers, Annabella's fingers fell away and Ryan took over completely. His touch was everywhere now—her temple, her throat, the curve of her breast. And all the while he kissed her as she'd never been kissed before—thoroughly, languidly, exquisitely.

It was heaven!

Leandra Logan is fascinated with both the power of angels and the convenience of babies arriving by basket. She decided that weaving them into a Temptation plot would be a delightful challenge. *Angel Baby* is the wonderful result—babies and the power of love are a natural combination! It is also the conclusion to her loosely connected baby trilogy including *Happy Birthday, Baby* and *Bargain Basement Baby*. Also look for Leandra's story, *A Bride For Daddy,* in WEDDINGS BY DEWILDE—an exciting new continuity series beginning in April 1996! Leandra would be happy to hear from her readers. Please write her at: c/o Harlequin Temptation, 225 Duncan Mill Road, Don Mills, Ontario, Canada, M3B 3K9

Books by Leandra Logan

HARLEQUIN TEMPTATION
393—THE LAST HONEST MAN
433—THE MISSING HEIR
472—JOYRIDE
491—HER FAVORITE HUSBAND
519—HAPPY BIRTHDAY, BABY
535—BARGAIN BASEMENT BABY

HARLEQUIN AMERICAN ROMANCE
559—SECRET AGENT DAD
601—THE LAST BRIDESMAID

Leandra Logan
ANGEL BABY

Harlequin Books

TORONTO • NEW YORK • LONDON
AMSTERDAM • PARIS • SYDNEY • HAMBURG
STOCKHOLM • ATHENS • TOKYO • MILAN
MADRID • WARSAW • BUDAPEST • AUCKLAND

For Ann Merkl Strommer
An old friend, who keeps our friendship
constantly fun and new!

ISBN 0-373-25664-7

ANGEL BABY

Prologue

Heaven

"MARGARET MARIE O'HARA is bound and determined to marry the wrong man!"

Guardian angel Annabella already knew this to be true of her lovely human charge, but stood graciously silent before her celestial superior Raphael: Two robed forms aglow in a white vastness, full of grace, but stuck with a dilemma.

Annabella had grown quite fond of the young, headstrong redhead who'd been under her wing since birth. She was Margaret Marie on the books, but to Annabella she was wild little Maggie, the image of Irish spark and spunk, with her emerald eyes, freckled nose and tempestuous nature. She'd grown and matured into a good woman of whom Annabella could be proud, an ethical attorney who always struggled to do the right thing.

Fortunately, Maggie's goodness made it possible for Annabella to hover near, to envelop Maggie in a protective, radiant light.

Unfortunately, however, Maggie wasn't much for introspection. A heck of a scrapper who leapt from one cause to another, she was impervious to Annabella's telepathic suggestions.

After twenty-eight years of custodial hovering, Annabella was still on the outside looking in, and Maggie's stubborn, impetuous spirit had landed her in a huge jam. Maggie was in conflict with fate, was at a crossroads with her destiny. She either had to answer Annabella's call to real joy, or permanently veer off into an uncharted future.

In short, Maggie was stumbling around down on the earth below, making chaotic decisions about her personal life, decisions which would wreck everything!

Annabella's existence was no piece of cake today, either. Raphael was about to strip her of her most cherished guardianship, and take Maggie away forever!

The Book, a directory of the world's souls, suddenly appeared suspended in the space between them. Pages scrolled with calligraphy flipped through the air at the archangel's psychic bidding. The parchment fell open at the proper page in the Os.

"Margaret Marie O'Hara," he proclaimed. "Daughter to Helen and Sean O'Hara, born February 17, 1967, breech birth."

"Difficult since the beginning." Annabella sighed.

"Leading with the wrong end by nature," he argued. "Despite this trait, it has been your job to keep her on the right course, Annabella."

"Maggie has followed her fate in many ways," Annabella pointed out. "She is a successful attorney who has righted wrongs for many, regardless of their circumstances, from the rich and powerful to the poor and helpless."

"Indeed," Raphael concurred. "But the picture is not complete on the personal side of the ledger. Margaret Marie O'Hara is betrothed to Timothy Richard Ryan. Together they are to beget Mary Margaret Ryan in the upcoming year!"

Annabella thought of little else these days. "I have tried to bring the pair together. But Maggie is so involved in her work, and seeing Owen Fortescue on a regular basis—"

"That unfulfilling relationship has gone on far too long!"

"What would happen, say, if Maggie were to marry Fortescue instead?" Annabella ventured hesitantly.

"It would disrupt the earth's balance for the next century."

"But Raphael, she only has eyes for him."

"She isn't consulting her heart on the matter," Raphael objected. "Ryan hasn't had a chance! Margaret Marie hasn't even noticed him yet."

"I have attempted to bring them into proximity numerous times—"

"With no success!"

"You can lead a lady to water..."

"But you cannot make her drink," he finished. "Yes, I acknowledge your heightened efforts in response to the urgency of the situation. You've used the powers of nature and circumstance to the limit."

"If only she'd open up, just a crack, and let me fuel her intuition."

"Of course it would be intolerable to interfere with any human's free will," Raphael stressed, understanding the temptation tugging at Annabella. "But it is believed that if this pair were thrown together, the proverbial sparks would fly."

Annabella had pulled every metaphysical string she could think of to bring the couple into contact and stir up the natural attraction now lying dormant. Why, at this very moment, Ryan was occupying the office right below attorney Maggie O'Hara's in downtown Boston's Bremer Building! But they moved in their own separate worlds, passing in the lobby, but never connecting. Six months under the same roof, and they hadn't communicated at all, aside from taps. Maggie tap danced on her hardwood floor to relieve her stress and Ryan hit his ceiling with a broom handle in an effort to relieve his. Some romance.

"About Timothy Ryan's guardian angel David—" Annabella began.

"David is busy with other charges who need him desperately," Raphael broke in, "and Timothy Ryan isn't the sort who requires lots of angelic care and tending. He's a bit of a hardhead, and a bit unkempt, but he's full of joy, humor and wisdom. All to his credit, Annabella. He loves people and deserves the opportunity to father Mary Margaret, raise her as the Ryan she should be. No, the burden of connection lies with Maggie and you, as her celestial companion."

"But what if Maggie continues down the wrong path with Owen?"

"Then she will be robbed of her chance at motherhood, Annabella. For you see, it is written that this particular vein of the Fortescue bloodline will most wisely cease with Owen."

"Oh."

Raphael sent the book floating back into infinity. "Of course, Margaret Marie O'Hara wouldn't even know what she had missed," he admitted wistfully. "She would continue to do the marvelous work she does in the name of justice—"

"But Maggie would be forever cheated of the delights her child would bring!" Annabella lamented.

"And the world would be cheated of Mary Margaret Ryan—a tragic loss to mankind," he added. "We've big plans for little Mary, who promises to be a firecracker with Margaret's drive and determination and Timothy's keen insight. Mary is destined to be a powerful negotiator in the world's struggle for permanent peace. A diluted version of her personality could handle the mission, but the blend of the rich Ryans and the O'Haras' bloodlines is just right."

"Please don't take Maggie's custody away from me, Raphael! Give me one last chance. I'm sure I can set it right."

"I am hoping that another angel can ignite a spark in Margaret before it's too late. Become the companion that you—"

"I am her companion! As it is written!"

"We have our higher goals. The common good must be our foremost concern."

"I'm certain no one else could've done more," Annabella maintained. "And I am telling you now, I'm willing to take the most drastic action possible!"

"Visit earth as a human? Is that what you are proposing?"

"Yes, of course! A human in need," she wheedled sweetly. "Maggie can't resist someone in distress."

"You haven't taken human form since that stormy September night in France in 1781, when Benjamin Franklin was about to trip in front of a horse-drawn carriage and die before his work was done on the peace treaty with Great Britain. And even then you only appeared for a short while, walking the street, waiting to keep him from harm's way. Remember, Annabella?" he challenged. "You fell into a gutter gushing water. He mistook you for a thief! I had to come down myself in the role of your father! Chilled me to the bone." His robed figure of light shuddered at the memory.

"I'd hoped to blend with the ladies of the night surrounding me," she said defensively. "In two-hundred-year-old hindsight, I realize that I should have taken the shape of a burly man, strong enough to handle the weighty Franklin without arousing suspicion."

"Regardless, we are not well equipped for making the transition to flesh. We are meant to stay in our own dimension and transmit our work through real people."

But Maggie couldn't hear Annabella's transmissions! And the idea of losing her altogether without a fight was intolerable. "I admit to a clumsy rescue back then," Annabella said. "But I've observed a lot in the past couple of centuries. I won't make the same mistakes this time."

"Still, Annabella . . ."

"I'm not arguing the challenges of appearing on earth in a human body. But the rewards in this case would far outweigh the discomfort, and be twofold."

"Obviously you would work to bring Maggie in touch with Timothy Ryan. But what else could you possibly want to do? Have some of that chocolate confection you so loved the last time?"

Annabella laughed, sensing his impending permission. "I want to take on the tiny form of Mary Margaret."

"The baby? Why?"

"It would be Maggie's opportunity to fall in love with Mary, as well as Ryan. What better way to prepare her for the future and insure her cooperation than to tempt her with a glimpse of family life?"

Raphael's demeanor grew lofty. "We don't normally offer test spins, like an automobile dealership."

"With all due respect, I think we will have to be flexible, if Maggie's fate is to be properly realigned. She is a visual person, one who has to see what she is missing."

"Babies are the most helpless of creatures, Annabella. You would be bound to the environment, vulnerable to the elements."

"It's bound to be uncomfortable, and risky. But a baby's state of helplessness gives it an awesome power. One tiny cry for help has adults jumping through hoops."

"If you could manage to get Margaret and Ryan jumping through the same hoop, it would be profound progress," Raphael conceded. "They are bound to click, being a match made in heaven. I suppose I can grant permission for a brief visit to Boston."

Raphael's inflection on the word brief troubled Annabella slightly. "This could take some time."

"A few days should be enough to get the fire lit. That's all you can expect to accomplish, without tampering with their free will. Rest assured, faith will set the course. We all need our faith."

"I will need other things as well," Annabella mused. "A basket, a blanket. A note of introduction."

"It can be arranged."

"Oh, yes, and a real dollar."

"For the chocolate, Annabella?" he asked dolefully.

"No, to pay my retainer! Maggie would be obligated to turn me over to the authorities if I'm not her client."

"Excellent point."

"Then I may proceed?"

"It is supposed to storm in Boston tomorrow. Just your sort of traveling weather!"

"And yours, I hope, Raphael. Surely you won't mind giving me a lift? Down to Massachusetts?"

1

IT WAS a dark and stormy night in Boston.

On that Thursday in mid October, Maggie O'Hara was working in her law office on Tremont Street, oblivious to the passing of the early evening hours. It wasn't until her antique grandfather clock chimed nine times that she drew her attention away from the land agreement she was drafting for an old and prosperous client long enough to realize that a new and less fortunate one was late. Very late.

She eased up out of her soft leather chair, stretched as far as her wrinkled royal-blue suit would allow and ruffled her mass of curly red hair with stiff, tired fingers. The only light burning was the brass lamp on her desk top. It was powerful enough to cast a glow on the face of the old German clock in the corner. She'd made no mistake in counting the chimes. It was nine o'clock. The client was an hour late.

Maggie worried when people missed appointments. It hadn't happened much during her three years as an associate with the firm of Gimble, Wethers, and Dushane, located across the Charles River in Cambridge. Their average client arrived early, full of pomp, circumstance and demands. But since she'd branched off into her own practice on Tremont, in the unpredictable Boston Common area, she never knew what was going to happen. The four-story Gothic-style brownstone where she occupied a top floor office was a fine example of Boston's posh antiquity, but lacked the formality of her former firm. This was deliberate on Maggie's part. Tired of zestless corporate cases, she'd hungered for a variety of legal challenges.

Maggie popped a chocolate truffle into her mouth from the cut-glass candy jar on her desk as she sank back into her chair. She slipped the land agreement papers back into their file folder, absently noting that her secretary, Jenna, had attached the label to the flap upside down. She smiled and reminded herself that she'd hired the nineteen-year-old especially for her people skills and spontaneity. She'd sensed that Jenna was someone who would welcome the unusual as Maggie herself did. And in the year since its inception, the law firm had gotten its desired share of the unexpected.

Maggie frowned at the frosted-glass door dividing her dim inner office from the brightly lit reception area as she waited for the house phone on Jenna's desk to buzz, signifying the arrival of a visitor downstairs. Despite her thirst for adventure, she still valued punctuality. In her experience lateness often led to real trouble.

But hadn't Maggie anticipated complications from the outset of this case? The client was a referral from a county social worker, Emma Campbell, and Emma had insisted that the woman's identity be kept confidential, at least until Maggie had agreed to take the case. Maggie had not refused to take the case, but because she perceived herself to be a good judge of character, had insisted that the woman herself call to set up an appointment.

The voice on the telephone had been youngish, but without a girlish lilt, and had sounded frantic. Maggie had pressed her for details, but she'd been too frightened to reveal anything. Still, Maggie'd gotten some insight. The woman's grammar was far from pure, but she was a good enough communicator to persuade Maggie to stay on after business hours for this meeting. And she had a quick wit, she'd hedged with short, blunt phrases as Maggie'd tried to elicit snippets of information about the case.

Maggie had guessed that this mystery client was streetwise in a way that she was not; accustomed to taking care of herself, but smart enough to know when she needed outside help. Maggie had grown intrigued enough to stay behind, despite the fact that her socially well-connected parents were having a dinner party tonight in their Beacon Hill home for some visiting French aristocrats, a colorful congressman from Texas, and a presidential aid who had recently taken a bullet for the Commander in Chief himself.

Maggie could tell by her mother's tone that she hadn't taken the last-minute cancellation at all well. Helen O'Hara had even insinuated that perhaps it had been unwise to give Maggie some of her inheritance in advance to cover the first year's rent for the brownstone office. Maggie was extremely sorry to hear this, for she had another birthday coming up and sincerely hoped for another injection of funds. Asserting her independence had proven costly, what with all the expenses of establishing herself, and then taking on some eccentric clients who had neglected to pay in full. It was wonderful at times to be from a stinking rich family, but only when the money wasn't wielded like a club.

But in the end, Helen's opinion and her veiled threats hadn't mattered one iota. Maggie always did what she deemed best for business. For whatever else the spirited, impetuous Maggie was, she was also thoroughly dedicated to her job. So here she sat, munching on chocolates while the elder O'Haras and guests ate their way through Rock Cornish hens and the cook's legendary cranberry sauce. Not really a bad trade-off, she decided, sinking her teeth into another piece.

But where was her Ms. X?

Maggie spun her swivel chair around toward the window as a tremendous rumble of thunder played the prelude to an astonishing flash of lightning. For a long moment it was as though the blackened sky had split wide open, sliced in two by a huge golden bolt. She dashed to the window, and with hands propped against the sill and her nose within an inch of the pane, took in nature's spectacle.

She wasn't certain how long she remained riveted by the sight before a noise in her reception area jolted her back to reality.

Maggie moved swiftly toward the connecting front office wondering how her very late client had managed to bypass the security lock on the door downstairs. As she swung open the door she heard a slight murmur and extending her hand, said "Hello, there—" Her salutation dissolved in a cry of surprise as she stopped short and stared at Jenna's colonial desk. A huge wicker basket sat between the telephone and appointment calendar and inside the basket, snuggled in a pale yellow blanket, a baby lay sleeping.

Was the mystery client's problem centered around this child? Or perhaps she had not been able to find a babysitter. Maggie wheeled around the small opulent room, searching for an adult to complete the scene. There was no one else!

Suddenly the baby squeaked and Maggie realized that the voice she'd heard moments ago hadn't been a grown woman's, but a babyish gurgle. She self-consciously dropped the hand she still had poised in midair and stared down at the miniature person, a girl, judging by its frilly white bonnet and pink suit. Despite its squeaks the baby was still breathing evenly in slumber, russet lashes the color of Maggie's own fanning her chubby cheeks.

Maggie quivered with an overwhelming sense of helplessness. For the first time in her privileged, checkered life, she was alone in a room with a defenseless baby! But wasn't she just as defenseless? she reasoned with rising panic. She had absolutely no experience with infants.

Well, the baby had to have been delivered by somebody, and that somebody couldn't have gotten far. With fresh determination she grasped the basket firmly by the handles and transferred the baby to the sofa in her dim inner office. She then closed both frosted-glass doors behind her and took up the chase.

All five of the other offices on the top floor were locked up tight. In the gloomy hallway Maggie glanced left, then right, then back again, torn between the small elevator and the open staircase. The car at a standstill on the ground floor suggested that her visitor had never climbed aboard, so the stairs seemed like the wiser bet.

Maggie charged down the hall as fast as her tight blue skirt would allow, and made a hard right turn onto the stairs. She grasped the black iron railing and peered down the hollow space to the lobby floors below as her pumps skimmed the worn stone steps, hoping for a glimpse of someone ahead of her.

Her heart leapt in her chest as she spotted a flutter of white fabric on the second-floor landing. She simply had to catch up with this person. Get some answers. Give that baby back!

Maggie picked up the pace until she was almost moving at bannister-sliding speed. She came to a skittering halt in the cool, dimly lit lobby, however, dumbstruck to find it empty.

It just couldn't be! Charged with frustration, she clenched her hands at her sides. The lobby was deep and narrow, with the staircase tucked off in the back. The person just ahead of her couldn't possibly have run through the lobby and out the door that quickly.

A shiver coursed along her spine. It was as if her visitor had vanished into thin air. Maggie raced for the entrance, bracketing her arms to shove open the glass door with force. She rocketed outside into the driving rain and into the arms of a rangy-looking character dressed in a tight black T-shirt and faded blue jeans. Talk about circumstantial evidence—he had a white sweatshirt tied round his neck and was carrying a roomy wicker basket. Furthermore, the basket held a pale tumble of fabric, similar to the one upstairs....

"Hey, where's the fire?" he complained, righting himself against the impact. Maggie steadied herself on the sturdy, damp forearms clamped around the basket.

"We need to talk, mister."

Their gazes locked in mutual recrimination as they instinctively crowded underneath the building's front awning to avoid the rain. Maggie couldn't help but note how striking his keen blue eyes were, how sexy the stray lock of black hair looked tumbled across his forehead. But none of that was important at the moment, with an abandoned baby in peril!

Timothy Ryan's lean, whiskered face flushed under her scalding look and royal tone. After he'd lived for six solid months in the same building with this fascinating woman, it figured she would finally notice him on his way out. His lease was up and he was in the process of moving his belongings out to his car. This was a fine farewell from the building's most beautiful tenant: Her eyes were drilling him with emerald-chip intensity, and she was digging through his things!

Maggie's little freckled nose scrunched as she stood on tiptoe to examine the contents of his basket. It wasn't identical to the one upstairs, but she couldn't help wondering if he was some kind of wacko dropping off baby bundles.

What she originally thought was a blanket, however, proved to be a fluffy towel, and the basket smelled a whole lot like garlic and sweat socks. Maggie released a heartfelt sigh as she paused in confusion. It was highly unlikely that this was a second nest for a sweet-smelling baby like the one upstairs, but her intuition was screaming that this man held the key to something. The moment the pads of her fingers had lighted on his sinewy arms, she'd felt an electric shock singing her insides that bonded them together in a disturbing fusion.

"Is there something you want?" he inquired dourly.

"Well . . ." She faltered, not sure how to express herself, "are you—"

"Am I wet? Am I busy? Am I trying to get back inside?" He rattled off pertinent possibilities in glib retort. He'd often wondered what it would be like to talk to her—among other things. But he'd never mustered the nerve to make that all-important initial play. She was an uptown babe who rode the elevator and he was a back-street guy who preferred the stairs. Oh, how he would've liked to have trailed her up the stairs just once, while she was dressed in one of those tight skirts of hers....

Six months ago he'd moved into an office on the third floor just below hers. In the beginning he hadn't paid much attention to her, but as his lease dwindled away, the crazy dreams of her had begun. She became the star of his unconscious late show and he woke up many a morning determined to make contact. But her power walk through the lobby had always put a realistic spin back on things quick. She'd looked right through him, not even flinching under his most flirty smile, irresistible to most women between the ages of sixteen and seventy.

And she really wasn't available, as he'd originally hoped. More than once he'd spotted her on the arm of some guy almost old enough to be her father. But he wasn't her father. He'd seen them kissing in an elevator car one day as the doors were swooshing shut.

Ah, well, the games were over, anyway. He'd been bounced back into the street, back to the North End, his original stomping ground. He'd almost escaped with his dream version of her intact, the image of her as a captivating Venus with a heart of gold. But she was too uppity, and too bossy to click with him. Imagine, digging into his laundry basket without permission, and searing him with a look that seemed to want to strip him, not of his clothes, but of his secrets.

With a disgusted sound he tried to edge by her to the door, but she continued to block his path.

"I'm looking for the person who left something in my office—"

"I've never been to your office," he assured her curtly. "And I'm in the process of moving out of mine. So if you don't mind . . ."

She eyed him skeptically. "You have an office here in the building?"

"The key word is *had*."

He probably was telling the truth. She had seen him around on occasion—cruising through the lobby in his grubby clothes, trotting up and down the stairs. She'd assumed he worked for a messenger service.

"You remember me," he challenged. Almost ran over me in your high heels a few times, he silently added behind his broad, cynical smile.

"This means you're really not the one I want!" she gasped in dismay.

"Well, boo-hoo." He pushed past her and hooked the door handle with his fingers.

"Did you see anybody in white come charging down the stairs in the past few seconds?" she demanded frantically. "Right before me, I mean."

"I've been hauling stuff for thirty minutes," he paused to report. "And nobody could've gotten past me on the steps."

"Did you see anybody leave this building?" she grilled.

"Nope."

He obviously wasn't the person she was looking for. What a foolish waste of her time, she inwardly fumed. Maggie shook her head to clear her mind, then shifted her attention to the sidewalk and street, to search for the white figure. There were two people dressed in yellow raincoats on foot across Tremont and that was it. She stared at the drenched cars rolling along the slick asphalt, headlights piercing the darkness. The Common across the way was dark and wet, and seemed devoid of life. The only stationary vehicle in sight was a big '70s-model maroon Impala with a cream vinyl roof. It was illegally parked in the loading zone just beyond the awning with its orange hazard lights flashing. She rushed into the rain to peer inside.

"You're wasting your time, you know," he called as she cupped her hands against the passenger-door window.

Maggie's wild mass of red hair flew as she whirled to find him slouched against the threshold, propping the leaded glass open with his athletic shoe.

"And just how the hell do you know? This could be the getaway—the very car I'm looking for."

"Naw, that's my car."

She glared at him through the downpour as she scurried back under the shelter of the awning. It figured. This character would drive an old tank. And have just enough nerve to double- park it.

"May as well face it, you imagined the whole thing."

"What?" she screeched, raising her fists.

He shrugged with languid indifference. "You dozed off in your office and dreamt that you had a visitor."

"I don't sleep on the job and I sure don't put much stock in dreams—" She cut herself short, wondering why she was bothering to bicker with him.

He took one last look at her, remembering just how sweet an illusion she'd been. "You'd be surprised how colorful and realistic dreams can be."

She turned her back on him, and gazed up and down the street.

"Hey, I'm tellin' you," he called out again in one final attempt. "Nobody left the lobby ahead of you."

"There had to be someone! That baby in a basket didn't just fall out of the sky."

"Baby? You dreamt about a baby?"

"It's no dream!"

He made a thoughtful sound. "And you thought I had a baby in my basket too."

She wrinkled her nose. "Until I smelled the sweat socks."

"It's my laundry basket," he hooted defensively. "Whadaya expect?"

"I expect nothing," she claimed icily over her shoulder. "I only know that we can't both be right about my visitor."

"So I'm wrong," he deduced.

"Does it matter? I thought you were on your way out," she reminded him with a false smile.

"Won't be long now," he assured her gruffly. He opened the door and stepped inside.

Maggie squared her shoulders with a disgusted mutter and marched back into the lobby in his wake.

Timothy's heart did a crazy somersault as her heels clicked behind him on the stone floor. He'd been so annoyed when she'd ignored him on their previous encounters and now that they had finally connected, it was under such insulting circumstances. She'd actually suspected him of dumping babies off in baskets! What a nut case.

He exhaled to gain some control. It didn't strain his detecting skills much to conclude that he was even more irritated with himself for still finding her so damn attractive. But he couldn't help himself. Even now, he veered toward the single elevator, to take what he considered a lazy man's mode of transport, just to prolong this encounter.

Maggie plunged into the car after him, breathless and frustrated. She put a hand on the wall panel, and noting that he hadn't punched in a floor, inquired "Can I hit your button?"

Timothy wanted to tell her that she couldn't seem to stop hitting it, but he swallowed the dry retort and set down his basket. "What are you going to do now?"

"Attack this problem from the other end, of course," she proclaimed, jamming her left thumb into the Door Open button.

He rewarded her with a patronizing look. "The baby."

"Yes," she brightly confirmed. "You oughta be a detective."

"I am a detective. Private," he explained with a smile worthy of the most fatherly family physician. "Maybe I can help . . ."

She flashed him a deprecating smile. "Help with my imaginary problem?"

He raised his hands in a loose-jointed movement. "Call me flexible."

"I don't think I'm going to be calling you at all."

"Why not?"

"You're not my type."

"You have a type of detective? Who has a type of detective?"

With her thumb still pressing the Open button, she turned around to meet him squarely. "I prefer ones who have long-term leases," she pointed out.

He'd sidled closer with his hands shoved into the back pockets of his old jeans. With a jumping pulse she backed into the gold handrail. She inwardly conceded that he was extremely attractive in an unkempt way. He had a boyish charm marred somewhat by a measure of cynicism. Perhaps life had hardened him around the edges.

"I don't know you at all," she pointed out.

"The name is Timothy Ryan," he offered with a twinkle in his eye.

Maggie tugged at her royal-blue jacket distractedly. He was Irish too, just as she'd suspected from his slight brogue and fair skin. But sharing the same heritage wasn't enough reason to give him the benefit of the doubt. And touching him, gazing directly into his eyes, had her feminine intuition flashing orange every bit as brightly as his Impala's hazard lights. Strange, considering that she'd frequently passed by his loping figure without a tremor.

"You must know my uncle Patrick," he pressed. "He's a cop who works this area, sometimes even walks the Common beat."

Maggie's full red mouth parted in surprise as she made the connection between the men. This was Patrick Ryan's capable nephew, Timmy boy? The one he was always bragging about? Boston's answer to Philip

Marlowe? Patrick had painted such a suave, unrealistic picture of him. Timothy Ryan wouldn't blend into the scenery enough to spy and probe for her kind of corporate client. He'd be questioned for vagrancy within an hour!

"How do you suppose I could get away with parking my car out front if it weren't for Uncle Pat?" he challenged in the gaping silence.

She gave him a stiff sidelong glance as he sidled up to her on the left. He held up a wallet he'd extracted from his back pocket. "See? I'm exactly who I say I am."

She sighed hard and accepted the wallet he was pushing in her face. Everything was in order, she had to admit. She slowly flipped through the plastic sleeves, studying the contents with increasing interest. "Ryan, I do know your uncle. And he's mentioned that you're an investigator."

He released a relieved breath. "I'm sure Patrick laid it on pretty thick—"

"It took a 'dozer to push the bull away." She struggled to control the smile twitching at her mouth as she handed back the billfold.

"Yeah, but I've even done some work for other tenants in the building, like Ed Flanders, the insurance agent, and Rodney Barnes, the plumber."

"Really? What did you do for Rodney?"

His expression was openly wounded. "You know better than anyone that that kind of information is confidential!"

"Just testing," she confessed airily. She was mildly curious about the unassuming plumber, but she was far more interested in whether or not Ryan believed in client confidentiality. He'd passed with flying colors.

That, plus the enlightening peek into his wallet made this scruffy private cye a gift from heaven tonight.

It wasn't merely his credentials that had sold her, but the plastic-sleeved pictures of Timothy Ryan balancing small children with the ease of a professional juggler. They were hanging all over him with bright toothy smiles, obviously delighted to be in his company. And he'd cherished the moments enough to keep the photos with him, taking up space that could've been filled by overextended credit cards and pictures of voluptuous bimbos.

Maggie released the button holding the doors and pushed the one marked four. Somehow she had to get him into her office. It might seem underhanded to use him as a go-between with the baby, without giving him a full explanation. But she knew his flirty, wiseacre type. He'd laugh her out of town if he discovered that someone smaller than her three-foot yucca tree frightened the daylights out of her! Besides, allowing him to believe he was scoring points with his skills and charm was nothing short of a favor to his ego.

Her pulse picked up tempo as his arm grazed her jacket sleeve. But to her dismay he was pushing the button marked three. Was he really giving up so easily?

"So you still think I was dreaming about the infant," she challenged with new flirtiness as the elevator creaked upward.

"'Fraid so," he insisted with a slow shake of his raven head. "I'd like to humor you for the sake of a business contact—"

"Humor me?" she repeated in disgust.

He sighed. "Unless the kid can walk, it just can't be up there."

"I saw someone fleeing on the stairs."

"I suppose somebody could've slipped onto the third floor," he conceded. "I left the fire exit open—"

"No, this person was already on the second landing as I started out on four."

"No way!" he snorted, rubbing the back of his neck.

She attempted a snort herself, but it was more of a sniffle. The elevator stopped on three. He picked up his basket, and nodded as the doors slid open. "Sweet dreams."

Panic struck like lightning as he brushed by her. He was really getting off—the only person standing between a helpless child and scaredy-cat lawyer. She should just admit her frailty. But his blue eyes had been so mocking beneath those long, sexy, black lashes. "I'll just bet you one hundred dollars that there's an abandoned baby up in my place," she blurted out to the broad expanse of his back.

The ploy worked. He back-stepped into the car with the grin of a carnival hawker homing in on a mark. "Going up."

As the ancient elevator creaked its way to the top floor, Maggie almost felt guilty about the trick. Almost.

She led Ryan and his basket down the hallway to her office. "I sure hope you have a hundred dollars on you, Ryan," she said merrily over her shoulder.

Timothy had about twenty dollars in his pocket, and no place to bunk that night aside from the back room of his parents' North End pizzeria. But she would never have a chance to call his bluff. He was dead sure of his

facts and she undoubtedly was flighty enough to con-
fuse fantasy with reality. Why, her mood swing in the
elevator proved that. She'd leapt from arctic to coy.
Flipping open his wallet had seemed to trigger the
meltdown. Maybe that picture on his driver's license
had a basic sex appeal. He'd have to take a long hard
look at it later on....

Maggie whisked open the door to her office and
breezed through the room en route to the next. Timothy paused to read the lettering on the frosted glass:
Maggie O'Hara, Attorney At Law. Then he sauntered
into the reception area and dropped his basket and the
sweatshirt loosely knotted around his neck on a green
leather couch. No babe in sight, he noted, looking
round the room which, except for the posh furnish-
ings, was similar to his own on the floor below. Come
to think of it, his former office was located directly underneath hers. Which meant, coincidentally, that they
had been indirectly communicating with each other for
quite some time.

"Hey, I already know you," he called out as he moved
toward the inner office. "You're the tap dancer."

She was squeezing her damp russet hair with a pink
handtowel as she peeked out the door. "Huh?"

"You're the mad tapper," he repeated. "The one who
stomps the length of her floor with remarkable, but
annoying rhythm."

"Why, to know that, you must be..."

He smiled and nodded. "The ceiling rapper."

"I'm not inconveniencing anyone," she scoffed. "I
only dance after hours."

"Well, I'm a night owl," he grumbled, not about to
admit that he had occupied his office 'round the clock

during his six-month tenancy. Judging by the quality of her suit and the antique furniture in her office, Maggie O'Hara was not hurting financially.

"Your opinion of my dancing doesn't matter anymore, now that you're moving on, does it?" she reasoned cheerily. "Nice bonus to my hundred."

"Your—" He broke off with a hoot. "There can't be a baby up here."

"Come see for yourself," she invited with a crook of her finger.

2

"I'LL BE..." Tim released a soft whistle between his teeth as he gazed over Maggie's shoulder into the basket on the desk. Somehow, some way, a baby had been delivered here.

Maggie could feel his large hands squeezing her shoulders as he craned his neck for a closer look. Thank heavens he was interested. His voice was a deep, gentle coo as he greeted the groggy infant.

The little girl was irresistible, even to a rookie like Maggie. Her eyes had opened the moment Maggie had hovered overhead, and those round hazel gems had been fastened on the lawyer ever since. She was enchanting, with deep dimpled cheeks, a cupid bow mouth, and burnished curls that peeped out of the edge of her white-eyelet bonnet. Despite being abandoned, she looked well cared for. Her cap and dainty pink suit were spotless and her creamy skin smelled sweet and clean.

Suddenly her arms and legs began to flail and she made a whiny sound.

"Are you talkin' to us?" Tim purred, grazing her curved cheek with his finger.

"How old do you think she is?" Maggie asked.

"Oh, I'd say between seven and eight months," he wagered, hooking his finger under the baby's chin.

"Look, there's something clutched in her hand." Maggie grasped the fat little fist in an effort to extract the paper from it. To Maggie's surprise, the baby didn't want to give it up. "It's almost like she's trying to fight me for it," she murmured, kneading the tiny fingers open with the pad of her thumb.

He chuckled. "Yeah, sure. She likes her privacy."

Maggie shot him a sour look. "Ha, ha." The paper proved to be a cocktail napkin. "It's from the Colony Club," she noted in surprise, turning the blue-and-red-striped square in her hand. "It's a very exclusive place," she added thoughtfully. "So much so that it's a little mysterious."

"No place for this little treasure," Timothy declared. "She belongs in a cozy crib with a stuffed animal parade."

"You, ah, want to pick her up?" Maggie asked hopefully.

He cocked a thick black brow. "Don't you?"

"I want to check out her nest," she explained defensively.

"For an owner's manual, maybe?" he taunted mildly.

"For any clues to her identity," she snapped, feeling to see if anything was hiding within the folds of the blanket. "This is serious, Ryan. Abandoning a helpless child . . ."

He could sense her fear. He didn't mind playing along, though. This was what he'd been after all along, an entrée into Maggie's life, a chance to get to know her. It was the only way he could make a fair comparison between his dream image of her and the real thing. Besides, he was nuts about babies. He was an uncle several times over. And as he approached the thirty-year mark, he longed to be a father.

Maggie released an audible sigh of relief as he reached into the basket and closed his hands around the child's middle.

"Come here, darlin'," he said with an exaggerated groan as he hoisted her up over his head, then fit her snugly into the crook of his arm. Using his free hand to untie her bonnet, he peeled it off to expose a wild mass of curls almost as red as Maggie's.

Maggie swallowed her envy at his easy, magic touch, and busied herself with an inspection of the basket. To her relief, the baby hadn't come empty-handed. She made a verbal inventory as she produced each item. When she held up a plastic bottle full of apple juice, she got an instant reaction from the baby.

"We'll put that to use right now," Tim said, clucking understandingly. He edged his lean hip along the edge of the massive oak desk and tipped the baby into his biceps. "C'mon, Maggie, take the cover off the nipple first," he scolded playfully. "My hands are full as it is."

Maggie's faintly freckled complexion reddened as she popped the protective cap off the bottle and handed it over. Tim inched the rubber nipple between the baby's lips and she began to greedily draw in juice with deep suckling noises.

"Okay," she sighed, dipping back into the basket. "A handful of disposable diapers."

"That'll last a couple of minutes," Tim retorted.

"One silver locket on a chain."

Maggie's announcement brought a startling cry of complaint from the baby, who instantly began to squirm and whine.

"Maybe she doesn't want you messing with her jewelry," Tim teased.

"It's as though she really has something to say," Maggie marveled, watching her intently. "First she didn't want to give up the napkin, and now this fuss about the locket."

Tim rolled his eyes, shifting the baby in his arms. "That's silly."

Maggie pinched open the oval-shaped piece to reveal two pictures set side by side: a handsome, but hard-looking man in his forties with dark hair and piercing eyes, and a woman who looked to be about thirty with a brassy blond dye job and a large painted mouth. The photos weren't the posed sort one expected to find in a romantic piece of jewelry, they were rough cutouts from a larger photograph. Judging by the slices of background, they were clipped from the same picture.

"Looks like the lovebirds were put together in a hurry." Timothy voiced her thoughts as she angled the locket toward him.

"Ever see either one of them around the building?"

"No."

"Same here." With a huff of frustration, she set the locket on the desk beside the napkin. She was amazed to note that the wee one was tracking her every move intently. Even when Maggie's hands were again tumbling through the basket, the child's eyes remained focused on the silver necklace. But the baby couldn't really be thinking about that piece of jewelry. Could she?

"You'd be amazed at how often babies made a sound or cast a knowing look at an opportune time," Timothy said, reading her awed expression. "It's just a fluke."

With a dismissive "Hmm," Maggie continued her search. "Hey, here's something—an envelope." Maggie peeled it open to find a single sheet of pristine paper folded three times. Maggie opened it up and a single dollar bill fluttered to the desk. "You need me," she read aloud. "And I need you, for just a little while. Keep me safe. Love, Annabella."

"Hey, that's cute," Tim said, planting a kiss on the baby's downy forehead. "Nice to meet you, Annabella."

Maggie frowned pensively, studying the letter. The stationery was good quality, the blue ink was from a fountain pen, and the cursive lettering was flawless. "I just don't get it," she murmured, staring off into space.

"Get what?"

"The photo in the locket matches the voice of the client who set up tonight's clandestine meeting. But this type of letter doesn't seem like her style."

Tim leaned over for a look. "It is pretty formal. Ah, but people are weird."

She regarded him dolefully. "That's your explanation, Mr. Private Eye?"

His eyes crinkled at the corners. "Hey, I like that 'Mister' stuff. Haven't been called Mister since Sister Clare in the fifth grade. And she was pulling at my ear at the time," he confided with a painful wince.

"Pulling at your ear?" she repeated blankly.

"Yeah, we were on our way to the principal's office to discuss my frog. Somehow it ended up in her cookie box."

Maggie envisioned the scene with a grin. "Well, surely you can detect the meaning of this, can't you?" she said, picking up the bill and waving it in his face.

"That your services are the cheapest in town?"

"No, it means that Annabella is my client," she corrected. "That whoever wrote this note was shrewd enough to make the distinction between abandonment and employment."

"Ah, so you won't have to turn her over to the county, you mean," Tim surmised.

"Right." Maggie slid the bill through her long slender fingers with a thoughtful expression. "Despite the formality of the letter, the woman who was supposed to meet me tonight struck me as clever enough to arrange this situation."

"The person in white?"

With a shrug Maggie leaned into the desk. "Well, I guess so. I try to limit my assumptions on any case. Wrong ones often lead to useless dead ends. This lady would know how the county works, however. It was a social-worker friend of mine who recommended me to her in the first place."

"Interesting." A fleeting frown crossed his lean features. "You know," he said thoughtfully, "there *was* somebody else in the building."

"What!" Her cry was sharp enough to draw a whimper from Annabella. Maggie gave the baby's curly head an awkward pat. "Sorry, kid."

"Guess I overlooked her because she was coming in, rather than going out," he hastily explained, taking the empty bottle from Annabella. "And she was dressed in a dark trench coat."

"What about her build, her coloring . . ."

Tim held the baby against his chest and rubbed her back to encourage a burp. "She was all bundled up. Her coat collar was flipped up around her chin, and she wore a scarf over her hair. She made a beeline for the elevator."

"She could've been a frightened client trying to evade detection."

"Or she could've been a woman shielding herself from the rain, a tenant who forgot something in her office," he countered.

Maggie shrugged in frustration. "What time?"

"About ten minutes before I ran into you."

"That might have been my client! You should've told me right away."

"She wasn't wearing any white," he pointed out, shifting Annabella back into the crook of his arm. "When you said you were looking for someone leaving, dressed in white, I didn't even consider her."

Maggie waved her arms. "Now I'm dealing with two separate people."

"I doubt it. There are twenty-four offices in this building. My guess is that the trench-coat lady is an uninvolved tenant."

"Nobody hangs around here at night," she objected. "But on the other hand, she must've had a key to the entrance. That would prove that she's a tenant."

"Uh," he gulped, cuddling the baby closer, "I sort of let her in."

"A stranger!"

"It wasn't that cut-and-dried. I was pushing open the door with my basket, carrying a load of stuff out to the Impala . . ."

"And she scurried frantically inside, as though she didn't have a key?" Maggie finished. "That would indicate that she was a visitor."

"No, I had the door propped open for a minute and she smoothly eased inside. I had hauled everything into the lobby and was transferring it to my trunk all at once. That's how I know exactly who was coming and going at that time."

"Well, you didn't see my figure in white come or go," she pointed out.

"Then that person is a tenant," he deduced.

"But the lady in the trench coat didn't have the baby with her," Maggie reminded him. "Somebody had to bring the baby!"

"Well, it's no use popping a garter belt about it."

Maggie was in no mood to forgive a chauvinistic remark, no matter how lopsided a grin the offender was wearing. She grasped Tim's T-shirt, curling the knit fabric between her fingers, and pulled his face inches from her blazing green eyes. "I should take your hundred bucks and a few chest hairs."

He swallowed as she flicked her polished red nail over some of the coiled black curls at the neck of his shirt. "That's another thing we need to discuss—the bet. Would you consider taking it out in hair?"

She gasped in furious realization. "You don't have the hundred dollars?"

"I didn't think I'd lose!" he shot back defensively. "Guess there's a first time for everything."

"I doubt if it's your first time at losing." She looked pointedly at his old clothes and tousled hair as she released him.

His mouth curled sardonically. "Oh, I've lost plenty of times. But I know my women—figuratively speaking," he added, inspecting her generous curves. "I had you pegged as the stubborn, know-it-all type who would never admit to a catnap, never accept that she might have dreamt up a baby."

Her curly hair flew in a long banner of red as she tossed her head indignantly. "I know I am not a know-it-all."

"See what I mean? You know for sure, don't you?"

She burned under his attack. She was so angry that she forgot her fears concerning the baby and scooped her up from his lap. "C'mere, darling Annabella," she crooned into the soft curve of her ear. "We girls don't like to discuss our garter belts, do we?" To her embarrassment, Annabella's lower lip jutted out and she squirmed to reach for Tim.

He folded his arms and remained seated on the edge of the desk. "Sorry, baby," he purred, "but you weren't left down at my place."

"How can you just turn your back on a defenseless little girl?" Maggie chastised, as she wrestled with Annabella, who was kicking and twisting for freedom with a piercing cry.

"Hell, it's big girls like you that cause all the trouble," he complained. "You start out all cuddly and sweet, then grow up all bossy and quick-tempered."

"A terminally single man, I take it," she said sarcastically, setting Annabella back in her basket. A few minutes of tussling and she was exhausted. How could she hope to fulfill her obligations to the child? Not only was she inept in the nurturing department, but Annabella seemed attached to Ryan and only Ryan. This linked Maggie and Ryan in an awkward tango—if he felt any sense of obligation to the baby, that is.

"And you've been married?" he challenged, offended by her inaccurate shot. "Not likely. Any woman with enough free time to tap-dance the night away all by herself is a woman who needs a social life."

Maggie set her hands on her hips angrily. "Like you're in demand? I'll bet the society columnists would like to get the inside scoop on social giant Timothy Ryan—find out how much gas your twenty-year-old Impala burns, and just which you spread on first, the peanut butter or the jelly."

"I hate peanut butter," he grumbled. "And, some people think I'm a damn interesting character," he added, extending his lip in much the same way that Annabella had.

"No question," she promptly agreed. "Consider the ear mystique surrounding you, Ryan. Just how and when did your one lobe grow longer than the other? A trendy treatment in Switzerland, perhaps? If you're shrewd, you can put that glib genius of yours to work adding gusto to your lackluster Sister Clare story, transposing the incident from the classroom years ago to a clinic tucked away in the Alps."

His expression grew concerned as his fingers stole to his left lobe. "Is one ear really longer than the other?"

"You are impossible to insult!" she lamented, dropping into her expansive leather chair.

"Don't underestimate your prowess," he said ruefully, moving his hand down his bristly jawline.

"Well, you had a lot of nerve assuming I was hallucinating about the baby," she pointed out. "You were ready to take a hundred dollars away from me—"

"The bet was your idea!"

She pursed her lips. So it was. But her pride prevented her from telling him that the money had never been of interest to her, that all she wanted was help with Annabella. She'd rather he viewed her as an opportunist like himself, than an incompetent. But it seemed he already suspected she was a washout with wee ones. And she had pounced on him after learning that he was broke. What a fine beginning.

She tossed her rich, disheveled hair over her shoulder. How had their bickering gotten so out of hand? The energy between them seemed to have taken on a life of its own, as though they were old, old friends who delighted in getting to each other. That phenomenon was as strange to Maggie as the mysterious abandonment. Surely their meeting wasn't fated, despite the instant sparks between them. After all, she had a man in her life, Owen Fortescue. And she wasn't high and dry with this baby; there were other people who could help her with Annabella. Annabella might not like any of them as much as she liked Ryan, but her mother had a houseful of help for the baby to choose from! Common sense told her that this man had nothing in common with her, that any involvement with him would be impossible.

"Okay, so maybe it would be fair to call this deal a Blind Billy," he reluctantly conceded.

Maggie had heard the Irish term before, but wasn't certain of its exact meaning. But she was going to find out!

"I shouldn't've pretended to have a hundred dollars to stake," he went on. "I just liked the banter between us and didn't want it to end. This being my last night, I might never have seen you again."

"But you would've taken the money had I been wrong," she insisted.

His sensuous mouth curved with annoyance. "Yes, I would have. Out of need. You seem quite well-off by the looks of things," he observed, gesturing to the grandfather clock and the leather furniture.

"How did you ever end up in this building?" Maggie couldn't resist asking.

"Amazingly, I won a six-month lease in a contest sponsored by the Boston Better Business Association."

Her creamy forehead furrowed. "How odd."

"You mean, how unlikely," he corrected with a keen sparkle in his blue eyes. "Does seem strange. Don't even remember entering. It's probably due to my mother. She enters everything."

"How is the private investigation trade, then?"

"It has its ups and downs," he admitted, leaning across the desk to graze Annabella's cheek with his finger. "Most of my old clients wanted nothing to do with my new place—found it uncomfortable and suspicious. And there haven't been many new ones to replace them."

"Well, you can go back to where you came from," she said genially.

If only it were so! If only he'd thought that far ahead. "One good client on the long term would've been enough to get me going here," he suggested.

Ousted on his rear, defaulting on a bet, and he was trolling for work in the final hour! What a hustler. "I have an arrangement with an agency on Bowdoin," she informed him evenly.

"And they will understand all about Annabella's circumstances? Your need for secrecy for the sake of the frightened mother, your wish to keep her in your care as the note asks you to?"

"Well, I do want to keep Annabella under wraps until I find out who she is," Maggie admitted, biting her lush scarlet lip.

"I don't think we should just part ways—there are too many signs that fate is at work," he said coaxingly.

She flashed him a wary look. "What signs, Ryan?"

He struggled for something solid to satisfy her legal mind. "Our tapping to each other. Our bumping into each other."

"Sounds like a lot of inconvenient collisions to me," she objected.

He gritted his teeth behind a smile and rose from the corner of the desk to pace around the room. If only she could see herself through his captivating visions! "And there is Annabella's attachment to me," he added smugly.

She was affronted by his inference that Annabella liked him best. He was right, but he still had a lot of nerve, charming her little charge.

He brightened suddenly. "I think I have just the deal for you," he announced. "If you did hire me to help with Annabella's case, I could work off the hundred with my services. Only after that would I start charging you."

"I have the feeling that this case is going to be charity work," Maggie returned, her eyes moving to the tired baby. Annabella had been batting her long russet lashes in an effort to stay awake. Maggie saw her own fighting spirit in the child. She couldn't help but feel that

Annabella had some sense of what was happening, that she was struggling to monitor their conversation!

"Well, maybe you could give me a bit of office space in return for my services," he suggested.

She picked up a pencil and twirled it with her fingers. The cad had an idea. She'd have to pay a lot to engage her regular agency to look into the situation. And, as Ryan had pointed out, they might feel obligated to report Annabella to the county. Understandably, they were careful to protect their license.

He moved closer as her expression softened in the lamplight. "So what do you say?"

She laughed into his anxious face. "I say okay. On the condition that you keep your needs minimal here in the office. I have other cases to attend to, and my secretary Jenna is already extremely busy—" She cut herself short, wondering if she was inviting disaster.

"You won't even know I'm here," he guaranteed.

"Okay," she relented.

"So you think you can manage the night without me, then?" he asked mildly.

"Manage the—" her voice cracked when she realized it was not a sexual innuendo, but a question concerning the baby.

"I have a document to deliver," he explained. "It can't wait."

"Serving a subpoena?" she asked in all certainty.

"No job too big, no job too small, Maggie."

"We'll get an official start on the job tomorrow morning." She rose from her chair to shake his hand. "Good night, Ryan."

"Good night, Maggie." He clasped her hand firmly in his own, unable to resist stroking her pulse point with his thumb. "And good night to you, charming Anna-bella." He dipped down to kiss the baby's temple, wishing he could do the same to her temporary guardian. "I know Maggie's in a hurry now, anxious to get to the store to buy you all the things you're going to need."

Maggie's eyes widened and her jaw sagged. He had her again.

He mercifully went on addressing the sleeping child. "You know, more diapers, more bottles. Formula, the premeasured liquid kind, of course. And some jars of solid foods—a fine variety of fruits, vegetables and meats. Apple juice goes without sayin'. Maggie knows you favor that. Blankets and clothes will probably have to wait till tomorrow," he said, putting her bonnet back on her head. "I'd sit with you myself tonight if I didn't have my errand. As it is, you'll just have to go along with Maggie."

Maggie kept a casual pose near the connecting door as he paused in the reception area to pull his white sweatshirt over his head and grab hold of his basket. The second he was gone she raced back to her desk and jotted down every item he'd mentioned.

THE EMPLOYEES and regular customers in her neighborhood supermarket gave Maggie curious looks as she moved through the bright, busy aisles. She frequently shopped at this time of night, but she rarely took a cumbersome cart, and it had never held a basket with a snoozing baby!

She'd never noticed before just how noisy the store was. Clomping feet hit the floor, disco music filled the air, checkout scanners bleeped. And everything creaked, from the wheels on the carts to the stock boy's dollies.

Thankfully, most of the baby items were consolidated in an area marked Baby Headquarters. Maggie dug into the pocket of her forest-green raincoat and glanced over the list. Vanity prevented her from keeping the paper on display after she'd noticed that the two other women in the section apparently didn't need one. They were loading things into their carts without the slightest hesitation. Maggie joined them with a front of brimming confidence. Ryan had exaggerated a little when he'd called her a know-it-all, but she did like to appear totally capable at all times. She tried not to wrinkle her nose at the tiny jars of whipped peas as she added them to her cart. They looked like yucky green mud.

Maggie lingered a couple of extra minutes until the women moved on, then moved to a shelf displaying childcare books. She grabbed anything with a grinning baby on the cover. Maggie had some things on her side in the baby battle, such as her insatiable curiosity and her unquenchable thirst for information, not to mention her speed-reading skills. By morning she'd know what to do and when to do it. She'd be the most capable know-it-all Timothy Ryan had ever met!

Anxious to get home to her cozy bed for a snooze and some studying, Maggie went to the shortest of the three checkout lines. By the time she realized it was a cashier she knew quite well—sixtyish, stoutish, loudish Viola Schull—it was too late to back away gracefully. "Evening, Vi," she greeted as she began loading her items onto the moving belt.

"Hello, Maggie," the woman responded brightly, her broad face full of curiosity. "I never realized that you—" She broke off, as she thought things through. "You were never pregnant. This can't be your little girl."

"Just baby-sitting," Maggie explained in a whisper.

Viola reared back in amazement. "Really? You've never struck me as the type to take on such a task. With your career and all."

Maggie lifted her shoulders beneath her coat. "First time for everything."

Viola pulled each jar and bottle over the scanner with a shake of her gray head. "I suppose you have diapers already," she said suddenly.

Maggie gritted her teeth. She'd forgotten those. But in her own defense, they hadn't been in the Baby Headquarters.

"I'll just call back for some," Viola suggested.

"Yes, please," Maggie said in a grateful hush. "Better make it a big package."

Viola mouthed, "Okay, dearie," as she pulled the microphone beside the register to her lips. Maggie lurched in horror as Viola boomed into the mike with the energy of a torch singer, easily drowning out the background strains of Donna Summer. "Attention, stock man! A customer has forgotten her diapers here on old track number three. Would you be so kind as to hightail it up here with a Jumbo Junior pack of forty-fours? The pink pack, being that the baby is a female. Thank you so very much."

Maggie's eyes grew wide with mortification as she stared down at the snoozing Annabella, then back up at Viola. "Thanks a lot, Vi."

"Nothing to it, sweetie," she whispered back with a wink.

Maggie scurried out the automatic door soon after, as fast as her tight skirt would allow. Everyone within blocks now knew that she was caring for a baby. And that she didn't know what the hell she was doing!

Damn that Timothy Ryan for knowing so much! Damn him for niggling into her life! Especially damn him for abandoning her and her abandoned baby!

MAGGIE MANAGED to get the baby and her groceries back to her elegant Beacon Hill condo without mishap. By the time Annabella was fed, diapered and down for the night, it was nearly twelve-thirty.

Nine hours until her reunion with Timothy Ryan.

The realization that she was anxiously counting the hours was a shock to her system, just as his overpowering masculinity and charming double-talk had been. This distance between them was good, she decided practically, moving toward her small study with her new baby books in hand. It would give her the chance to do some childcare research in private, and do a final check into his background, via her personal computer.

It was nearly three o'clock before she hit the sheets of her queen-sized bed for some sleep. Her head was spinning with new information on basic childcare and the life and times of Ryan. The on-line background check had proven that he was exactly what he seemed: an honest, down-on-his-luck private eye, from an old Boston-based Irish family. He had two older sisters with families and Officer Patrick Ryan was indeed his uncle.

She couldn't remember ever being this energized over Owen Fortescue, the forty-four-year-old accountant that she'd been dating for the past two years. Steady, dependable, restrained in temperament, he had always seemed a good counterpart to her rapid-fire way of doing things. He was her brakes, her advisor—and her *father figure*, a small inner voice sometimes suggested.

True, her father Sean was a classic example of the absentee breadwinner. A brilliant professor at Harvard, who'd devoted his life to his work, he frequently lost himself in the past as some historians did. He was a rousing success, having published several popular Irish chronicles. But despite his love for his only child, Sean hadn't been there to guide and enjoy Maggie.

She and her mother, Helen, shared the same spirit and fiery temper, but her mother, too, had always had her own agenda and had made the deliberate decision not to have any more children. Apparently bearing Maggie had been murder on her waistline and had put a dent in her social calendar for months and months.

Not that Helen didn't welcome Maggie into her whirl with the other university wives. Maggie had gotten a hell of an education in Life 101 before her tenth birthday. She could speak several different languages by then, as well as stuff her bra, apply startling makeup, flatter Europeans with correct protocol, and wash wine stains out of evening clothes in any emergency. Sean and Helen had always loved her to the best of their abilities, and expected that she would remain single, pursue a satisfying career and date men of their social status.

It was no wonder that she was lost with this baby! She'd never been allowed to act like a child herself! It was no wonder she was lost with the loose, reckless Timothy Ryan. She'd never been allowed to date anyone of his type!

How alarming and intriguing that she should be confronted with these two reminders of the voids in her life on the same night: a wary baby with a lusty cry and an earthy young male with a lusty look. She tumbled the puzzle through her mind as she reached out to switch off the bedside lamp.

Was fate trying to tell her something?

3

"YOU CAN'T DO that! Or that!"

Maggie opened her office door the following morning to find her young secretary, Jenna Kinny, delivering a verbal assault to an unfazed Timothy Ryan. With her thin arms flailing and her shaggy blond hair flying, the nineteen-year-old, in one of her wildly printed minidresses, looked like she was a dancing in a discotheque.

"Good morning, Jenna," Maggie called out in firm greeting.

"Finally!" Jenna whirled around, her face filled with relief. But one look at the baby in the wicker basket sent her into another tailspin. "So it *is* true!"

Maggie shifted her gaze to Ryan, who was stretched out on her green leather couch. He was dressed in the same faded jeans of yesterday, topped with a T-shirt that bore the name of a locally brewed ale.

Tim returned her inspection with one of his own, and approved her appearance with a low, sexy sound. Her gold double-breasted suit with a barrage of shiny buttons drew out the bright highlights in her mass of curly red locks. The striped scarf knotted at her throat, which had probably cost more than his last month's food allowance, was threaded with an emerald shade that matched her eyes.

"I—I don't know what Ryan has told you . . ." Maggie began in a stutter. She was speaking to the secretary, but to Timothy's delight, she couldn't seem to tear her gaze from him.

Jenna was about to burst, but had to defuse long enough to answer the phone. The caller wanted to make an appointment, so Jenna began to flip through the pages of the appointment calendar on her desk.

Timothy broke eye contact with Maggie and sat up on the sofa to check on Annabella. She was wide awake, her huge hazel eyes the size of saucers. She beamed at the sight of him and raised her chubby arms to be picked up. He scooped her out of the basket, cooed good-morning and sank back down on the sofa.

Maggie stiffened as she watched the laughing exchange between man and baby. So the chemistry was as strong as it had been last night. Maggie sighed in frustration. She'd been the one who'd studied the childcare manuals, who'd bathed and fed Annabella, who'd propped her on her lap and pushed icky hot cereal into her mouth, over and over again as the baby pushed it back out. In the end cereal had been smeared everywhere. It had taken her forever to get them both presentable.

And she didn't want to think about the mess she'd left behind at her condo—a half dozen dishtowels full of cereal and juice and formula heaped on her counter; and the soiled skirt in her bedroom, the bottom half of the red suit she'd originally planned to wear today. Apparently those diapers didn't trap every leak, as they claimed.

Then there was the chocolate stain on the living-room rug. She rolled her eyes as she thought back to that miracle of cunning and motor skills. She'd set Annabella on the floor for mere seconds to run her bath and the baby had crawled to the cocktail table and grabbed a two-dollar truffle out of the candy dish. She'd gnawed it to a slobbery mess with her two front teeth all the while chirping about "cho-cho." Okay, so the stain was more saliva than chocolate, but her cleaning lady was going to complain. And she wasn't accustomed to sharing her candy with anybody!

And to add insult to injury, Ryan appeared to be inspecting Annabella for signs of slipshod service!

"I dug up a car seat and a diaper bag full of essentials for you," he remarked, tipping his raven head toward Jenna's desk.

Maggie's features softened as she gazed over at the molded seat with the bright orange cushion and the quilted tote bag decorated with big yellow ducks. "What a nice gesture, Ryan. Thanks."

"I'm sure they're not as fancy as you'd like," he added defensively. "They're hand-me-downs, but they're clean."

"I do appreciate it, really," she broke in gratefully. "I'll only need them for a short time. They're just perfect."

"My big sisters, Kate and Therese, pass this kind of stuff between them all the time," he explained, tousling Annabella's curls.

Her brows arched with real interest. "Really? I don't know much about . . ." She trailed off, unsure of the proper term to describe her lack of family life. "About, well . . ."

"Sharing?" he finished with a smug twist of his mouth.

"That's not what I was going to say!" she retorted with renewed annoyance.

"There's a lot you don't know much about, Maggie!" Jenna flared, slamming down the phone on her desk.

Timothy appealed to Maggie with a regretful look. "I tried to tell the kid we're working together."

"It's true, Jenna," Maggie confirmed on a note of bewilderment. "It just sort of happened."

"Well, I can't believe you let this happen," Jenna jeered as she stalked to the door connecting the inner and outer offices. She whisked it open and then stood back so that Maggie would get the full impact.

It was enough to send Maggie reeling back a couple of steps. But she recovered fast and charged ahead for a closer inspection. Her private quarters looked like a secondhand shop! Fishing rods, skis, roller blades, and boots were on one side. Cardboard boxes marked "clothing" were stacked up on the other!

"You . . ." Her mouth went dry as she reviewed, then denied the obvious.

"Moved in," he confessed a bit sheepishly with one of his charming smiles. "Hoped you'd understand."

The phone began to ring again, signaling another busy day. Maggie instructed Jenna to take messages and escorted man and baby into her quarters. She closed the door with a solid thud, then whirled to face the giggling pair. Ryan sat in her comfortable leather chair with Annabella perched on his lap.

"So, did you girls have a busy night?" he cooed, tilting Annabella's back against his chest so they were both facing their hostess.

"Not as busy as yours, Ryan!" She stormed around the room, nearly tripping over his set of weights as she took a closer inventory of his belongings.

"I couldn't stay double-parked downstairs forever," he pointed out. "Even Uncle Patrick can't perform miracles."

She threw up her hands. "But you had to leave to serve a subpoena!"

"Oh, that was just down the street," he replied with a dismissive gesture. "At the Fox Hunt Pub. Once that was done, I had no place to go."

She placed her hands on her hips and leaned over the desk with an accusatory glare. "You really could've helped me a whole lot more last night, but you chose not to then."

"Look, I didn't know for sure the serving was going to be that easy," he claimed. "Nothing in my business is ever for sure."

Maggie narrowed her eyes warily. He was full of the blarney. But it was impossible to make too much of the issue when she was trying to put on a capable front. "I can understand how you lost your office lease, and how you are short on funds, but why didn't you just go back to your home last night?" Even as the words tumbled from her mouth, she knew the answer. She stepped closer, with pursed lips that Annabella mistook for playful. The baby reached out to grab her mouth. Maggie captured her fingers and kissed them.

"Aren't you two getting along just dandy," Ryan noted in an obvious effort to change the subject. "See, all you needed was some time alone, just the two of you."

"Why were you living in this building?" Maggie asked sweetly. "Surely you had a home before winning the contest."

"I did," he assured her with a nod. "But when I won this palace of a place for six months, I went overboard. It put my shabby apartment to shame, you see."

"How careless!"

"It was a gradual decision," he explained. "I began to spend more and more time in my office because it was so comfortable, with its reliable heating and cooling system, and fine rented furniture. When my apartment lease expired at the end of May, it seemed a crime to continue on in that dump when I could be here."

"No wonder you were complaining about my tap-dancing," she retorted knowingly. "Probably wreaked havoc on your little tête-à-têtes. And how on earth could you clean up? The bathrooms at the end of the hall don't have showers."

Timothy thought about a few of his all-night dates and he offered her a faint, smug smile. "If you've ingratiated yourself in the right circles, you can manage to get both, sometimes at once."

"Ah." She felt a hot blush creeping up her throat. She should have seen that one coming!

"Don't ask questions you don't want answers to, Maggie," he suggested softly.

"Okay," she agreed, leaning so close that she could feel Annabella's curls under her chin. "Let's stick to the really important stuff. How dare you camp out here without permission?"

His gleaming blue eyes widened under her reproachful look. "I thought we were going to be partners for awhile."

"Yes, but—"

"I will be spending most of my time here with you, anyway. The baby may be in danger. Have you thought of that, Maggie? That the mother dropped Annabella off here because someone else may be after her?"

She sighed into his face. "Yes, I did think of that, Ryan."

"So I'll be playing bodyguard as well as investigator."

She rolled her eyes. "So the hundred you owe me will cover about an hour, I suppose."

"It's gone," he affirmed, gesturing to the clock.

"That's ridiculous!"

"I'm teasin'," he confessed with a deep chuckle that made her insides tingle. "You're the one who's making an issue out of the bet. I'm not much for material wealth—"

"Obviously!"

His thick black brows furrowed in disapproval. "And obviously, Maggie, you are accustomed to pampering yourself with the best of everything."

"That's no crime! You liked your luxurious office space here—while it lasted."

He shook his head. The finer things were fine, as long as a person had solid, humane values to balance things out. Did Maggie have such a balance? With every passing minute he hoped so, because she was oozing into his system like a dose of sugar, making him fidgety and excited; making him want a real taste of her. Like a long, deep kiss for starters. Her mouth was so close, he was inhaling enticing traces of her minty breath.

"Yes, Maggie," he answered wistfully, "I enjoyed it as a temporary treat, graciously accepting that it would end."

"You sure scrambled up here fast enough to barter for an extension!"

Timothy took a deep breath. "Maggie, Maggie, can't you see that despite our different backgrounds we are merging to accomplish one single goal? The best interests of Annabella are all that matter. I'm here to help as a favor. No money need change hands."

"Yes, you're right." With a soft sigh she cupped Annabella's soft, chubby face in her hands.

"In return for my assistance, I'd like to stow my stuff here," he went on with a glorious smile. Maggie could imagine him smiling like that in those afterglow moments between the sheets.

She straightened her spine and compressed her lips, startled by the sudden mental image of him in her bed. What an operator. First it was his stuff and his distracting masculine presence invading her space, and now he was invading her thoughts with tempting visions of love-play.

Undoubtedly, he was accustomed to getting his way with shameless use of his careless charm. She couldn't help but be fascinated, but she also refused to be completely railroaded—no matter how sexy the engineer happened to be! "You can leave your belongings here for now," she told him. "But we'll take this thing one day at a time, agreed?"

"Nobody asked you for a six-month lease, Maggie," he chided.

"I have the feeling you don't wait to be asked for anything," she retorted.

"A shrewd judge of character, Annabella," he murmured in the baby's ear. "We must look out for Maggie O'Hara. She's from the right side of the tracks, but she's a scrapper."

Annabella tore her gaze away from the bowl of chocolates—just out of reach on the desk—to chirp in approval.

Moments later Jenna swung open the connecting door. "Emma Campbell is on line one," she reported in a clipped tone. "Seems a little out of sorts."

"Lots of that going around, Jen," Timothy said, grinning at her over Annabella's head.

"Nobody calls me Jen!" Jenna snapped and whisked the door closed again.

"Does she really dislike the name?" he wondered, rising from Maggie's chair so she could reach her large console telephone.

"No, I think she just dislikes you exercising squatter's rights," Maggie observed. "I don't even allow her to keep pots of petunias on the windowsills, because neither of us would dust them. And you . . ." She made a sweeping gesture to indicate all the space he was taking.

"I don't need much dusting," he teased.

"Yeah, sure." She eased into her chair and rolled it closer to the desk, then turned to Annabella who was squealing on Tim's lap. "Hush, little baby, this is my contact with the county and my missing client on the line."

"As if Annabella understands," Timothy scoffed. But the baby promptly fell silent as Maggie picked up the receiver and pushed the blinking button on the console.

"Good morning, Emma. No, I never did make direct contact. Hoped you'd heard something." She paused to shake her head at Timothy. "Look, is there anything that you think I should know about her? Anything urgent, I mean . . . Nonetheless, I think we should talk face-to-face. A locket was dropped off here in my office . . . No, I ran downstairs for a minute shortly after nine, and I found the necklace along with a napkin when I returned. . . . Naturally, I'm not certain that she left them behind. But you might recognize the photos inside. . . . Yes, a male and female. Both strangers to me." Maggie listened intently, then turned a page on her calendar pad to the current date. "No, I'm tied up this morning with a court appearance. How about one? Good, see you then." Maggie hung up with a pensive frown.

"Emma Campbell never heard back from Madame X?" Tim wagered.

"No." Maggie rested her elbows on the desk and rubbed her temples. "And Emma didn't mention word one about any baby."

"Sounds like this client didn't give her much to go on, either," Tim commented, shifting Annabella from one arm to the other.

"We'll find out more this afternoon." Maggie opened the pencil drawer in front of her and extracted a brush and a gold barrette. Swiftly, she gathered her hair at the nape of her neck and secured it with the wide clasp. She pulled her boxy briefcase off the floor and onto her desk and opened it with a snap.

Tim wandered closer as she dropped some of the files on her desk into the case. "Weren't you even going to tell us that you're due in court?" he asked with a wounded look that was matched by Annabella, in her own cherubic way.

"I'm not accustomed to answering to anyone," Maggie replied with a shrug of her padded shoulders. "Jenna's my only employee and she's either programming me with itinerary or reading my mind." She knew she was exaggerating Jenna's role, but she felt her independence ebbing away at an alarming rate.

"This isn't going to work without some straight talk," Tim cautioned. "You're just assuming that I can care for Annabella this morning."

Maggie released a small, patronizing sigh. "Isn't that part of the deal? Aren't you on duty from here on in, Ryan? Your way of repaying my hospitality, for paying off the bet—remember?"

His mouth formed a grumpy line as he squeezed the chunky arms that had tightened round his neck. He didn't have any intention of letting someone else care for Annabella, Maggie thought wryly, rising from her chair. He'd only done so last night to force her into a friendship with the baby. "Okay, Ryan," she conceded on a softer note. "I'm putting in a request."

"Of course we're set." With a pointed look he added, "A guy just likes to be asked, Maggie."

"So does a girl," she returned with a significant glance at his belongings. "Now that that's settled, how about discreetly checking with the police to find out if a baby girl has been reported missing?"

"Already discreetly done," he reported with satisfaction. "No one's looking for Annabella yet. And nobody knows that I looked into it."

The relief on her delicate features was obvious. "Fine."

"While you're away, I'll have those tiny photos enlarged," he offered. "It'll make it easier for Emma Campbell to I.D. them."

Maggie nodded, pleased. Maybe this strange partnership was going to work. "We need a cover story for the public, don't we? What are you going to say to your uncle the cop, for instance? He's bound to ask some questions if you run into him on the street."

Tim stroked his strong jawline. "His first question will be, 'Why did that lawyer run a check on you last night, lad?'"

Maggie fidgeted in surprise. "How did you find out?"

"The clerk at the station faxed a copy of the check to your office here."

"Oh." She had the grace to look a little embarrassed. "Can you really blame me, Ryan?"

"No," he said, staring down at his scuffed shoes. "But had I known you were still unconvinced, I'd have taken you straight over to Ryan's Pizzeria on Salem Street. Eased your mind over a nice hot meal, courtesy of the family."

"An Irish pizza parlor." She turned the idea over in her mind.

"Not as fancy as you're used to," he said a bit defensively, "but it's comfortable, with plenty to eat."

Maggie had no rebuttal for a remark that was so true. She was a culinary snob. But interfering relatives, not food, were the pressing issue here. "Ryan, I wonder if it would be better if we left our families out of this altogether."

"Oh, it would be better, if only it were possible!"

"Well, isn't it?" she pressed fretfully.

"I'm afraid the Ryans are an inquisitive bunch. Though, on the bright side, it makes me a good private eye and Uncle Patrick a good cop." He shrugged bemusedly. "Thought such curiosity was natural to all families."

"Not to the O'Haras," Maggie answered slowly. "My father prefers to discover things through reference books and my mother wouldn't take any interest in a girl not old enough to wear Chanel N° 5."

"Well, babies and gossip are embraced by the Ryans. Naturally, I already had to admit to my sisters that I'm connected with a baby, to get the diaper bag full of goodies and the car seat."

Maggie gasped. She hadn't thought of that. "What else did you say?"

"I told them that I was helping out a fellow tenant, but believe me, that won't hold 'em for long. And they've probably passed the word on to all the other Ryans, including Uncle Patrick."

"Last night even the regulars at the supermarket were curious," Maggie recalled with resignation. "Guess we're trapped into hiding Annabella in plain sight, behind a smoke screen."

"We not only need a story, we need a good one."

"I suppose we could claim that Jenna's taking care of Annabella," she suggested.

The connecting door swung open three seconds later. By the horrified look on Jenna's face, she'd obviously been eavesdropping. "Don't you dare, Maggie! People might think . . . well, that Annabella's really mine!"

"All right, Jenna," Maggie said, instantly backing down, "but please get to work." The moment Jenna closed the door, Maggie turned off the intercom connecting the offices. "So much for that idea."

"It should be your story, anyway," Tim pointed out. "You'll be caring for Annabella."

"Well, I guess I could say I'm helping out an old high-school friend," she said. "But believe me, it's far-fetched."

"Not if you relax," Timothy advised, "and express pleasure over having the chance to care for Annabella."

She tested a huge grin on him.

"Not very convincing," he judged with a critical cluck.

"Well, I'm a whiz at a courtroom poker face," she asserted, surprisingly disappointed in his review. "I'd look mighty foolish making an objection with a gorilla-like grin."

"I think it's something you can improve on," he answered. "We need a name, too, of the mother."

"Oh, yes." She bit her lip in contemplation. "It should be a real name. One my mother has heard, but someone she wouldn't have access to."

"Someone who can't afford Chanel?" he suggested dryly.

"Someone who wouldn't even recognize the scent," she topped without resentment. "Somebody distant, and unimportant in social circles. I know—Amanda Springer. Mother would remember her from the Fulton Academy's tennis team, but not too well, for she was middle class, there on scholarship. That's what we'll do, say that Amanda needed a sitter and called on me."

"Have a reason why ready?"

"I'll think like you and one will turn up," Maggie murmured confidentially with a wink, surprised to realize that she was beginning to enjoy his company a lot. "Let me just find that locket for you." As she rummaged through her purse, Tim moved closer with an outstretched palm. She turned over the necklace, and held his hand for a moment. "Please be careful with her, Ryan."

Her earnest expression was touching from the baby's point of view, but annoying from his. "I'm good, Maggie," he said quietly. "Really good at what I do."

Every fiber of her being told her it was so. If she didn't trust him, it would ultimately mean she didn't have faith in her own judgment. She grasped the handle of her briefcase resolutely and moved toward the door.

"Oh, Maggie, which photo processing place do you recommend?" Tim asked her slender retreating back.

She stopped and turned to smile. "You really want my expert opinion on that, a savvy shamus like you?"

He sighed with amusement and regret. "What I want is your credit."

"I have an account with Maxwell's on Chestnut Street."

His face clouded in disbelief. "He's a robber!"

"He's the best," she squawked. "I get what I pay for! One more thing," she added. "Make the trip easy on the both of you by taking a taxi. Jenna has petty cash in her desk for such things."

Timothy winked at Annabella as Maggie stalked out the door. "She doesn't know about the finer things at all, baby. Not yet she doesn't."

"Cho-cho." Annabella raised a hand to his face and gave his nose a tight squeeze.

"You girls and your one-track minds!"

MAN AND BABY hadn't been out on Tremont two minutes trying to hail a cab when a vehicle pulled into the loading zone before them. Unfortunately, it was black and white, rather than the desired yellow, and Officer Patrick Ryan was at the wheel.

"Told you we Ryans are a nosy lot," he mumbled, forcing a smile as his favorite uncle emerged from the driver's door. "Mornin'!"

"Glad to have caught you, Timmy," Patrick Ryan called out in a booming voice as he joined them on the sidewalk. His face brightened in amusement as he examined the baby in the red-hooded coat once worn by his own daughter a decade ago.

Timothy was frustrated to be cornered so soon. But he certainly couldn't have pretended not to notice the cop on the beat. Patrick was a mainstay in the Boston Common area, easily recognizable because of his towering figure, and the head of bright white hair that peeped out from beneath his cap. He was highly accessible as well, because of his sense of humor. One minute on the sidewalk with his uncle and Timothy felt his big-city anonymity stripped away. Passersby were greeting them left and right, acknowledging Annabella with compliments and curiosity. Maggie would have a rightful fit if she knew the baby was on display this way.

"Could we talk later, Uncle Pat?" Timothy suggested as an Episcopalian priest from the nearby cathedral paused to inquire about his elder's health.

"No!" Patrick's thundering denial put a halt to his nephew's hedging maneuver. Timothy stood obediently by while the priest spoke to his uncle. When the good father moved on, Patrick waved Timothy over to the trunk of his squad car. He lifted the lid to reveal a playpen and stroller.

"Wow! Thanks a lot!"

"All I ask in return is some answers." Patrick unloaded the mesh-sided playpen and leaned it against the back fender, then reached in for the collapsible stroller. "How about we go up to your office with this stuff and have a chat?"

"A chat?" Tim gulped, cuddling Annabella in the folds of his black leather jacket. "I'm in sort of a hurry, right now. How about you hold the baby and I run upstairs with the stuff?"

Patrick squinted into the bright sunlight, and leveled a finger in his nephew's face. "First a nice lawyer like Maggie O'Hara runs a check on you in the dark of night. Then you call your sisters at dawn, begging for infant items. Now you show up with a wee one in your arms—" He broke off with a chuckle as Annabella turned to close her little hand around his finger. "Even you, my girl, with your obvious feminine wiles, can't sidetrack me," he cautioned, kissing her velvet knuckles.

"Okay, let's go inside," Timothy relented.

"I'll carry these things up to your office—"

"That's the first revelation," Timothy told him. "I don't have an office of my own anymore...."

4

MAGGIE BREEZED BACK into her office about twelve-fifteen with her briefcase in hand, to find Timothy and Annabella with Jenna in the reception area. The baby was propped up in the car seat and Timothy was in the process of pushing whipped chocolate ice cream into Annabella's rosebud mouth.

"Cho-cho," Annabella cried, her small face alight with pleasure.

Maggie smiled, finding the protest leaping to mind difficult to express. "Ryan, do you think that stuff is good for her?"

"She ate a healthy meal first," he answered, his bright blue eyes flickering with a mixture of annoyance and attraction as Maggie sidled closer. She had a spectacular shape. He looked forward to seeing her in something other than a business suit.

"But the books say—"

"Books, Maggie? You've been reading up on the care and feeding of our little rug rat behind my back?" His look of exaggerated disbelief made Annabella giggle. She tried to touch his face with a chocolaty hand.

Maggie flushed self-consciously. "Okay, so you have me. I had to study up on the subject of childcare."

"It's not a crime to be ignorant on a subject or two," he assured her.

"You make it sound like it is," she insisted. "So what

if I am most comfortable absorbing information from textbooks? There's nothing wrong with that."

"No, Maggie, there isn't. It's your pretending to be informed, that's the problem."

She grimaced as he mouthed "know-it-all" out of Jenna's line of vision, then turned her attention to the state of Jenna's desk. The paper cups full of soda and wrapped sandwiches strewn all over it advertised the deli down the street.

"Ah, I see you found another establishment that takes my credit," she observed mockingly, grateful that there was a cup and sandwich reserved for her.

"Figured you wouldn't mind." Timothy stretched his long legs out over the plush red carpeting, exuding sinewy power despite his casual clothing. "Figured you'd want to reward Jenna with her lunch for watching Annabella while we're at Emma Campbell's this afternoon."

Maggie pulled up a straightbacked cherrywood chair to the side of the desk. "You don't mind, do you, Jenna?"

"No," Jenna replied with a fond glance at Annabella. "I baby-sat a lot in junior high. As long as you understand my clerical efficiency might suffer a little, Maggie."

Maggie pursed her lips, wondering how bad that could be, considering her upside-down labels and multiple clerical errors at the best of times. "I'm sure Annabella will nap at least part of the time," she ventured consolingly.

"I'll just run down to the bathroom for some water before you two leave," Jenna announced, rising from her chair. "Babies make lots of messes."

"Good idea," Maggie affirmed, unwrapping her sandwich. "I want you to keep this place buttoned up tight while we're gone. Answer the door to no one."

"Then I'll be down the hall a few minutes longer," Jenna amended, before easing through the door.

"Security will have to be tightened around here from now on," Timothy added, eager to expand on Maggie's sentiment. "Any chance of you clearing your calendar for the next few days?"

Maggie drew Jenna's appointment book closer to take a look. "This is Friday, which will give us the weekend."

"Yes, but what about next week?" he pressed, his features earnest.

"Well..."

"Maggie, security strategies are part of my domain, right?"

"Yes, I suppose so," she relented. "I certainly don't have the experience."

"You have to understand that we can't leave this place unlocked at all anymore. Even when we're inside. Why, even the lock you have isn't all that great. If this drags on much longer, you'll need a better one."

"That's fine. But my appointments—"

"Any more court appearances?"

"No..."

"Direct Jenna to clear your time," he insisted.

She studied Jenna's notations, then nodded. "There's nothing urgent here, anyway."

He released a sigh of relief, feeling as though he'd conquered Mount Everest. But there was another mountain staring him in the face.

"So, did you get the blowups?" Maggie asked. She peeked beneath the top of her crusty bun to find a delectable stack of roast beef smothered in shredded lettuce.

"Yeah, no problem," he said hurriedly. "We need to talk about something else, though. In private, before Jenna comes back."

Maggie lifted a soft russet brow. "What's the matter, Ryan?"

He fed Annabella another spoonful of chocolate ice cream. "Nothing too big."

"Then why is your lower lip trembling?"

He heaved a sigh, and jabbed the slender baby spoon into the cup. "Annabella and I ran into Uncle Patrick on the street. He was delivering a stroller and playpen."

Maggie understood the implication immediately. "So the Ryan telegraph service is in full operation."

"Afraid so. He knew about your check on me, and of course I had Annabella in hand, verifying her existence."

Maggie frowned at him over the rim of her paper cup. "Cut to the chase."

"I couldn't turn down the baby gear. He insisted upon bringing it into the building." Timothy turned his large palms up in a helpless gesture. "And I couldn't take him to my office anymore, because I don't have the key."

"So you ended up here," she prodded impatiently.

"Yes. At that point our story needed some window dressing. It had some holes in it, you see—"

"What holes?" she snapped.

He took a gulp of cola. "Like what we mean to each other. Why you ran the check."

"You are working for me!" she clarified succinctly.

"But on what case, Maggie?"

"Does it matter?"

"It did to Patrick. He rightfully assumed that we were probing into something concerning the baby."

"Oh, no . . ." She trailed off in trepidation.

"It seemed wise to keep Annabella and our relationship separate."

She chewed and swallowed. "Yes, of course! So you told him that, as he'd hoped, I finally hired you for an important case. And that Annabella belongs to a friend of mine. Sounds clear-cut to me."

"Stop and think," he urged. "It wouldn't seem logical for me to be working some big case for you in a professional capacity and also be helping out with your friend's baby as a personal favor, would it now? And what about all my belongings in the next room?"

"Did you have to give him the nickel tour of the place?" she asked in disgust.

"Jenna did it, complaining at the top of her lungs about the clutter." He searched her face in an effort to gauge her reaction. Her expression looked lethal. "There I stood, beside everything I own, with Annabella in hand, knowing that there were so many things I couldn't tell him—that we got together because of a bet over the baby, that I'm working off my hundred-dollar loss, that you feel with every inch of your heart and soul that the baby is a client. Duty and the letter of the law are fine lines to tread, and the truth is so tangled up here, Maggie."

She squinted at him through her lush lashes and dug her fingers into his muscled arm. "You untangled it for us though, didn't you?"

"I offered the only explanation that seemed to fit," he returned with certainty. "I said that ours was strictly a personal relationship. That there's no case pending. That we're seeing each other, and you kindly offered to house my stuff while I search for another place."

She gasped in indignation. "People will say—"

"We're in love?" he finished roguishly.

"How could you take all that upon yourself!" she squealed with a shake that scarcely moved his solid forearm.

"It was the best answer," he insisted steadily. "It explained why my stuff is stowed here, why I'm willing to help with a child not connected to your business affairs." His expression became very earnest. "Would you rather have him suspect there's a mystery surrounding Annabella and launch a probe?"

"Guess you did your best," she admitted. She released her grip on him and sank back in her chair.

"No, I did the best anybody could've done."

"Well, it'll be crucial to keep our families apart during this ordeal," Maggie cautioned. "My mother would never buy the romance angle, so I'll have to tell her a different story. Oh, who'd ever believe us together, though," she added despairingly.

Timothy gave her a strained smile. If she could step into his dreams for just a minute, she wouldn't ask such a question.

EMMA CAMPBELL'S OFFICE was located in Government Center, several city blocks up from Maggie's office where Tremont curved into Cambridge. The autumn wind was blustery and it was nearly one o'clock, so Maggie insisted on taking a cab. She used the short ride up Tremont to reflect on the cover story Ryan had given his uncle.

"I have a male friend already," she blurted out to his chiseled profile.

Timothy turned slowly, a smile forming on his mouth. "I've seen your friend. Reminds me of Phil Donahue."

"Well, yes," she admitted warily. "He's prematurely gray, like Donahue."

"Maggie, Maggie," he chided with a shake of his raven head. "That may have been accurate in both cases ten years ago. But old people are supposed to be gray."

Her mouth formed an indignant O. "Owen Fortescue isn't old!"

"His name is Owen?" he hooted. "Hey, there's a hip name from generations gone by."

"We are a splendid pair," she assured him coolly.

"There's a word Owen taught you—splendid."

"Mind your own damn business, Ryan."

His expression didn't change. "How old are you, Maggie?"

"Twenty-eight."

Timothy was horrified. "He's gotta be forty-eight."

"He's only forty-four," she returned in snippy triumph.

"It's my understanding people are clumped in decades after the forty mark."

She lifted her flaming head haughtily. "I wouldn't know."

"Ask your father," he suggested significantly as the cab lurched to a stop at their destination.

Maggie fumbled with some bills to pay the driver, and tried to control her fury. How could she possibly explain this situation to Owen? Maybe she wouldn't have to, she thought, tugging at her gold pleated skirt as she eased out of the cab under Timothy's attentive gaze.

They were both silent as they moved along the sidewalk to the broad staircase at One Center Plaza. When they reached Pemberton Square, Maggie led Timothy past the historic Suffolk County Courthouse to one of the newer plaza buildings which housed county workers like Emma Campbell.

She paused just inside the lobby. "This visit will be my responsibility," she announced. "For Emma's benefit, you are in my employ as an investigator. Not a boyfriend. Not a baby-sitter. Okay?"

She sucked in a startled breath as he reached up to graze her cheek with his thumb.

"Touch of talcum powder on your face," he explained.

"Oh. Thanks." She rubbed her cheek, wondering at the way her skin tingled where he'd touched her.

"Not that we can rub away the sweet baby scent between us," he went on wistfully. "Hopefully, it's just obvious to our own senses."

Hopefully, his tantalizing impact on her senses was another secret she could keep. His sexy charms and provocative touch were almost blatantly obvious, but oh, so effective.

Perhaps it was just the fact that he was so comfortable with his own masculinity that made her so uncomfortable with it. The men she knew were distant and controlled by nature, unaccustomed to taking a female's point of view seriously. This was one reason why Maggie never intended to marry. She didn't care for the idea of deferring to any man the way her mother did. Helen O'Hara frequently got her own way, of course, but it was through subterfuge. Maggie didn't like the marital games she'd witnessed over the years. They certainly weren't for her.

Amazingly, Timothy Ryan didn't seem to mind working for her, as long as he had the chance to express his opinions. He was alarmingly accessible, from his worn clothing to his engaging smile. Despite his huge ego, she was beginning to find his openness exciting.

But he wasn't part of her long-range plan, she reminded herself. She had resolved to put her career as an attorney first, and keep romance on a tepid back burner with the likes of Owen. He was a fine escort who didn't pressure her on any level. Her parents approved and welcomed him to all their lavish Beacon Hill functions.

It was imperative that Maggie not allow herself to be aroused by Ryan's musky scent, or his careless touch. It was crucial that she ignore the lurch in her belly whenever he cuddled Annabella. It was a taste of intimate family togetherness that she'd never been exposed to before. She wouldn't allow herself to hunger for such things. She didn't have the background to make such a triangle work.

"Anything else I need to know?" he demanded huskily, as though sensing her train of thought.

She struggled to keep her voice level. "No, Ryan. Come on. The office is right around the corner."

Maggie led Timothy into a room filled with desks and partitions, and alive with activity and ringing telephones. "There's Emma," she murmured, "at the coffee urn by the potted plant." Emma noticed them and gestured for them to follow her into the commotion.

At fifty, social worker Emma Campbell was a little too plump from lack of exercise, her shiny cap of hair a little too gray from her years of concern for Boston's less fortunate. She shared one receptionist with a group of her colleagues and her designated space was a cramped glass cubicle, with a hollow pressed-wood door that kept conversations private but didn't buffer all the office sounds. She pushed it solidly closed before introductions were exchanged.

Maggie knew Emma well enough to recognize the sincerity in her smile, but she couldn't help but feel a trifle surprised when the sensible woman removed her brown, owlish glasses as she leaned forward to shake Ryan's hand. In a crazy way it was verification of her own instinctive response to Ryan, Maggie reasoned. Ryan had an undeniable magnetism, despite his denim and leather and his empty bank account. It was natural for her to be attracted to him. It didn't mean they were a match, or that Owen was less appealing in comparison. It didn't. Really, it didn't!

"Thanks for coming over, Maggie," Emma said warmly, setting her glasses atop an open file folder on her green steel desk. "I appreciate your concern, considering the circumstances. Not only would this missing client be hard-pressed to pay you a fraction of your regular fee, but she's playing cat and mouse for some reason."

"I do think that she showed up last night," Maggie began, sifting through the facts she intended to reveal. "As I told you on the telephone, I was forced to leave the office for a few minutes, and when I returned I found a cocktail napkin and locket on Jenna's desk. I saw a figure on the stairs, so I followed. That is how I connected with Timothy Ryan here—" She broke off awkwardly.

Emma's brows lifted. "Really. How fortuitous—for both of you, of course."

"I happen to be between jobs right now, anyway," Timothy explained in a smooth professional tone, topped off with one of his disarming smiles.

Emma glowed, then excused herself to answer her ringing telephone.

Between jobs, was he? Maggie gave him a wry, sidelong once-over. It appeared that he was between everything. He had no home, and she was fairly certain that he didn't have a girlfriend. It must be uncomfortable for him, to have his stuff stashed in her office, and to curl up on her furniture for catnaps. So why was he doing it? He had a large family as backup, and now they knew—thanks to his Uncle Patrick—that he was homeless. So why was he sticking close to her?

Maggie had been so concerned with Annabella and her infant needs that she hadn't thought much about Timothy Ryan and his motives. His position could be exactly as it appeared, that he was simply swept up in the sudden tide of circumstances. Anxious to help the baby, fearful that she'd bungle the job, he'd moved in as caretaker.

But another possibility had seeped into her consciousness along the way, one that had undergone a rapid growth spurt since Ryan's cynical critique of her relationship with Owen.

Timothy Ryan had moved into her life for an intimate look at who and what she was.

It seemed incredible that a casual man like Ryan would go to such trouble. Or that fate would open a door of opportunity for him. But he'd made no secret of the fact that he'd noticed her moving through the lobby of their office building, and that he'd taken the trouble to find out about her. Had he found her that appealing from afar? If so, he had a funny way of showing it. He seemed to delight in giving her static. The same kind of static she so enjoyed giving him, she had to admit.

Emma was jotting down some notes on a tablet now, hastily terminating the call. "I'm sorry," she said, replacing the receiver. "This place is a madhouse today. Where were we?"

Timothy reached into the inside pocket of his black leather jacket for the photographs he had blown up to five-by-seven size. "Here are enlargements of the faces in the locket."

Emma held out her left hand for them, and reluctantly set her glasses back on her nose with her right one.

Maggie watched the social worker study one picture, then the other. "Well, Emma?"

"I've never seen this man before in my life," she commented, "but this is our woman, Maggie. She's the one I sent to you."

"The one who fled your office as well then," Timothy added excitedly to Maggie. In other words, they'd most likely found Annabella's mother!

Maggie tipped forward in her orange plastic chair with a no-nonsense expression. "Emma, it's time to give me a name."

"Well . . ." Emma trailed off uncertainly. "She asked me not to."

"She must've intended to speak to me last night," Maggie countered, even though she wasn't sure of any such thing. It had occurred to her that the after-hours appointment had been simply a ploy to drop off the baby under the cover of night, then flee without a word. But she wasn't above bending the facts a little to get at the truth. She couldn't conceal Annabella much longer. "The important thing here is that she has faith in me. Enough faith to have left me a dollar."

Emma blinked in confusion. "A dollar?"

"Yes, don't you see? It's a symbolic retainer, Emma. She's my client now. Officially."

"All right," Emma relented, digging into her desk drawer for a file folder. "Her name is Darla Faye."

Maggie swiftly took hold of the folder Emma reluctantly offered. She opened it on her lap to find a single sheet of paper inside. "This is it?"

"Yes, a brief report concerning our meeting, and my recommendation that she consult you."

Maggie scanned the routine report, then passed it to Timothy.

"She didn't even leave an address," he noted.

"Darla revealed precious little. She was here on a fact-finding mission," Emma explained. "Asked a lot of questions about jail terms, parole, the witness-protection program, even wondered how often people disappear on their own."

Maggie and Timothy exchanged a worried look that clearly reflected their mutual fear. Where did Annabella fit into all of this? Had Darla dumped the baby, then gone underground to avoid trouble?

Emma noted their distress, and her own face clouded. "This could be very serious, I see that now."

"Is there anything else you can give us to go on?" Maggie asked.

Emma slid a pencil through her fingers with a thoughtful look. "She seemed to have little faith in the system she was so curious about. Definitely not the type I normally see in here, with her thick artistic makeup, her bright flowing pantsuit, and lots of jewelry—large silver rings, earrings, and a pretty bracelet."

"You think the stuff was quality, Emma?" Timothy asked.

"I don't know," Emma admitted on an apologetic note. "Not my field."

"I know the locket is quality craftsmanship," Maggie announced with a confidence engendered by her privileged background.

"Show her the locket, Maggie," Timothy suggested. "See if it's a match for any of the other pieces."

"Good idea." Maggie dug into her purse, impulsively pushing the napkin deeper into the lining as she produced the necklace.

Emma studied the piece, squinting behind her lenses. "I'd say it's similar to her bracelet. No, I'd go out on a limb to say they're a set." She handed it back to Maggie. "You'd think a woman with a jewelry collection would have attorneys at her disposal, wouldn't you?"

"Darla sounded quite savvy on the telephone," Maggie pointed out. "She must have reasons for all her moves."

"What next, Maggie?" Emma wondered. "There's not much I can do, aside from reporting this incident to the authorities. But what can I possibly tell them? We don't even know that Darla is a missing person. And she didn't say she was being threatened."

"I'll—we'll," Maggie amended under Timothy's steady gaze, "do a little more digging." She rose to leave, promising to keep Emma updated.

"Didn't you say something about a napkin on the telephone?" Emma recalled as Maggie opened the door.

"Oh, yes—" Timothy broke off as Maggie's sharp heel jabbed his toes.

"It was a silly mistake," Maggie intervened with a laugh. "Jenna dropped it near her desk. We'll be in touch. Promise."

"WHY DID YOU step on my foot?" Timothy demanded on their return taxi ride.

She eyed him impatiently. "I didn't want to discuss the napkin with Emma, of course."

He shook his head. "That wasn't my question!"

"It was the only way I could think to stop you," she blurted out in exasperation. "I think it best to keep the county a few steps behind us. And I could tell that Emma was intrigued. Too intrigued."

"Well, let's work out some sort of signal between us for future messages," he scolded sternly. "Something far less painful."

"Oh, the longer we know each other, the easier it'll be for you to sense my intentions," she predicted airily with a flutter of her fingers.

"I don't think we're on the verge of any sensory breakthroughs," he returned curtly, knowing all the while that it was one of the biggest lies he'd ever uttered. But she was so unflappable, so determined to be absolutely right, he couldn't give her the satisfaction of knowing just how deeply she'd gotten under his skin.

Silence pervaded the cab's interior for the duration of the short trip back to Maggie's office.

Timothy hopped out immediately. Maggie lingered in the back, counting out change to the driver. When she emerged, she was wearing a determined smile. "So, Ryan, how do you feel about elbows? For signaling, I mean?"

"Nudge me with something softer," he suggested with an infuriating smile. "That's the way to send a guy sensory signals, Maggie."

To her surprise, he started walking down the sidewalk behind an older couple with a poodle. "Where are you going?" She raced in front of him, blocking his path.

"My car is parked around the corner," he explained. "I thought I would take the photo of our mystery man to the streets."

"Oh," she replied in surprise. "Good idea."

His eyes crinkled in the sunlight. "Thanks."

She set her fingers on his chest and pressed into the soft fabric of his T-shirt. He suppressed a shudder. She was doing it only to detain him, of course, but his system couldn't make the distinction. He was aroused by her touch, the flare of excitement in her eyes, the wild way her hair was flying in the autumn breeze.

"What about Darla?" she asked breathlessly.

He took a steadying breath. "Until we know Darla's position, it wouldn't be smart to openly link her with this guy."

"Oh, yes, excellent point! I suppose I could try to track her down," she decided after a thoughtful pause.

His mouth thinned as he turned over the idea. He realized his blessing would be just a formality to this headstrong woman anyway. "Well, don't be obvious about it, like you were with the check on me."

Her eyes sparked. "Ever occur to you that I was intentionally obvious, Ryan?"

A dangerous smile played on his lips. "To keep me in line, then?"

"Something very much like that," she replied smugly.

"Here now, I thought you were just obvious by nature."

"What!"

He grasped her sputtering, flailing form by the forearms, and lifted her clear off the sidewalk and out of his path. He planted her to his left, started to move on, then thought better of it.

Maggie gasped indignantly as he whirled to snag her wrist. "Just need something from your purse," he explained smoothly, opening the brass catch of her suede bag.

"This isn't the way to get expense money," she hissed with a tight smile to a passerby. "I might have to call on Officer Patrick Ryan to collar you." She reddened profusely when his long fingers drew the cocktail napkin out of her purse. "Can't hurt to flash this around a bit, either," he explained triumphantly, clicking the clasp shut again.

Maggie's features were pinched in frustration as he sauntered down Tremont like a careless hood. Pure female instinct kept her riveted to the spot, watching the unmistakable strength of his wide shoulders moving beneath his supple black leather jacket, and the play of solid muscle in his tight jeans.

She reached up to tame her wind-tossed mane. How could a man with little more than a dime in his pocket be so arrogant, so sure of himself? She'd been groomed from infancy to perceive money as the ultimate instrument of power. This man had none. And didn't have the good sense to be worried about it! It was a phenomenon she didn't understand.

For that reason alone, Maggie felt compelled to draw Ryan just a little closer. She wanted to know how he defied so many of the rules she'd always lived by, and seemed none the worse for it.

5

"JENNA! Where's Annabella?"

Maggie's composure evaporated when she burst into her reception area minutes later, to find Jenna busily typing at her computer terminal, the baby nowhere in sight.

"Your office," Jenna answered in a distracted monotone, and continued to stare at the screen through a thick curtain of blond hair.

"Alone?" Maggie squealed in fear, charging forward as fast as her high-heeled pumps would allow.

"Hello, darling!"

Maggie applied the brakes as she ran headlong into her mother and a blast of Janet Jackson. The fringed Oriental rug that covered much of the floor was rolled back in front of her desk, and Helen was seated on the polished hardwood, propping up the baby, who was dressed in a miniature sweatshirt and jeans provided by the Ryans, and drowning in Maggie's size-seven tap shoes.

"Hello."

"Wondered when you'd be back."

Maggie blinked in perplexity as she absorbed the touching scene: Annabella, as cute as a button, with a chocolate-rimmed mouth, wiggling round in the shoes, and squeezing the life out of one Maggie's truffles.

"We were just testing out our hoofing skills," Helen explained.

"Cho-cho," Annabella crowed in delight.

Maggie leaned over her desk to turn off the cassette player and noted that her candy dish was empty. "Annabella's had way too much cho-cho," she complained.

"Don't worry, Maggie," Helen O'Hara purred, reaching round to feed the child a small piece of the confection. "This is her first and only one. I ate the other two myself."

Maggie made a breathless sound, her hand stealing to her throat. "You dislike babies, mother. Always have."

Helen O'Hara raised her thin, penciled brows. "I know, darling, I know," she cooed in complete agreement. "But there is something utterly irresistible about this child." She gazed down in bewilderment at Annabella's russet crown of curls.

Maggie stepped closer to scrutinize her mother for signs of delirium. But Helen appeared to be her usual classy, composed self, dressed in a trendy black suit by Valentino, and an earring and necklace set by Harry Winston that made Darla Faye's locket look like a Crackerjack prize. As always, her shiny wedge of hair was rinsed a youthful auburn, her complexion was translucent and unlined even at age fifty-five, and her vivid eyes were the truest blue with the aid of soft contact lenses.

"Such an angel," Helen purred, peeling back the neckline of the baby's green top to nuzzle her downy shoulder. "I don't know why I think you're such an angel, but I do."

Maggie moved dazedly to a plastic box on the bookshelf for a moist towelette. "What is it you always say? Babies drool like sailors on shore leave and wet like them, too. Isn't that a direct quote?"

Helen took the towel from her daughter and cleaned Annabella's hands and mouth. "As usual, your legal mind is demanding a logical explanation. I simply cannot supply one. Somehow, Annabella is the exception. And she is almost a facsimile of you at this age. She—" She broke off to stare at her daughter suspiciously.

Maggie dropped to her knees to join them. "Mother, I didn't have a baby behind your back. How ridiculous."

"Jenna says this child is about eight months old. Let's see," she calculated, gently rocking Annabella from side to side. "This is October, so that would put her birth date sometime last March. We were in the south of France for several weeks at that time, for your father's break from school."

"Mother!" Maggie cried in affront. "I can't believe you think me capable of such subterfuge."

"All right," Helen acquiesced, coming as close to an apology as she ever would. "Perhaps it was just an enchanted dream on my part."

"But you don't like—"

"I don't like other people's children, sweetie," Helen interrupted with a pouty look. "That doesn't mean I would not go absolutely insane for a new little O'Hara."

Maggie stared at her, dumbfounded. "You never said so before."

"Didn't know it until I took Annabella in my arms," her mother confessed. "It's as though the baby is magical. Not that I would want to be called Grandma, or Granny, or Nana," she hastily cautioned. "Helen isn't that difficult to pronounce. Two syllables, Annabella. Hel-en." She took the baby's tiny hands in her own manicured ones, for a round of patty cake. The dimples in Annabella's cheeks deepened as Helen stumbled over a terribly flawed version of Little Miss Muffet.

Maggie's pulse rate increased as she absorbed this new development. How interesting to know that her mother could care for a grandchild, if she ever cared to produce one. But it was distressing to realize that Helen's interest in Annabella was more than perfunctory. The story she'd concocted concerning Annabella's parentage was now going to be scrutinized.

"So, Maggie, if this child isn't yours, who does she belong to?"

"I'm caring for the baby for an old friend from school," she replied, easing her tap shoes off Annabella's stockinged feet. "Where are her little tennis shoes?"

"The shoes are on your computer terminal. Who is the mother?"

"Amanda Springer. Remember? From Fulton's tennis team?"

"The one with the moustache and size-eleven feet? How preposterous!"

"I expect you to keep those kind of opinions to yourself," Maggie scolded. "Annabella can hear, even understand sometimes, I think."

Maggie was startled when Annabella, who was staring up at her, clearly poked out her tongue.

Helen's laughter rang through the room. "What a coincidence! Or is it?" she amended with interest.

"I really don't know." Maggie stood up and picked up the phone messages Jenna had left under her snow-scene paperweight. The glass globe was slick with saliva and the small square sheets of pink paper were all smudged with chocolate. She glanced sharply at her mother. "You two would make lousy spies. The fingerprints and spit are dead giveaways."

"Annabella loves to shake that globe and watch the snow swirl," Helen answered from the floor. "I think she was calling the skaters inside, 'coos.' And the messages just sort of scattered across the desk top. I thought I was helping, stacking them back up."

"But you didn't have to read them, Mother."

"Didn't I?" she flared. "You've been so busy lately, you've not volunteered information as you usually do."

Maggie was tempted to point out that Helen's motherly interest fluctuated from intense to nonexistent, but thought better of it. "You're holding my only news right in your lap, which brings you right up-to-date."

Helen's mouth thinned into a knowing smile. "Jenna tells me there's a new man in your life, too."

Maggie's gaze strayed to her grandfather clock as it chimed the half hour. "Well, she shouldn't have," she replied eventually.

"Judging by his hodgepodge of belongings scattered about this room, I'd say he's firmly rooted here," Helen noted disapprovingly.

"He's a private detective who lost his lease in the building," Maggie explained with a dismissive flutter of her hand. "We have a barter arrangement. In return for storage space, he's doing some investigating for me. That's all."

"Maggie," Helen coaxed, "tell Mother all about it."

And generally, Maggie would have obeyed such a request. But Ryan was so unique and new, she wanted to explore who he was, without any familial influence.

"When there is something to tell, I will," she promised airily.

"Were you off with him last night?" Helen queried suddenly. "Is that why you didn't join us for dinner?"

"No, I was expecting a new client, just as I told you," Maggie insisted impatiently. "As it happened, Annabella's mother showed up, too."

"Sounds like quite a night."

"It was, Mother, it was."

"How's Owen, darling?"

"Owen's darling," Maggie returned sweetly.

Helen's flawless face grew grumpy. "Very amusing, Maggie. We missed him at our table last night, as well. Always such a fine addition to my dinners. Up on all the latest political tidbits. A master at the stock market—"

Both mother and daughter started when Annabella interrupted the glowing tribute with a man-size burp.

"Thank you, baby, for reminding Hel-en, two syllables, that singing Owen's praises doesn't alter our plotted course. Owen and I are..." Going nowhere. She winced as she acknowledged the truth. But she'd known all along that Owen enjoyed the single life. Somehow, Ryan's rude remarks about her relationship with the older man were forcing her to scrutinize it and to question it.

That was a very annoying trait of Timothy Ryan's, the way he was daring her to question herself. As if he thought she needed to reevaluate and make some changes in her life!

"Hasn't Owen ever suggested marriage?" Helen asked suddenly.

Maggie threw her hands into the air. "I don't believe this!"

"Oh, all right," Helen grumbled. "I know he hasn't."

"And for that very reason, you and father have always considered him a wonderful match!" Maggie leaned closer to the desk to level a finger at her. "Don't you dare pretend otherwise. You've always been pleased that I chose the single life, and to concentrate on a career that you can brag about to friends—and rivals."

"I'm sure this fuzzy maternal feeling will pass," Helen predicted with a wistful sigh.

Maggie wasn't sure she wanted it to pass. The idea that her mother would embrace a child of hers was surprisingly gratifying. "Just do try and keep Owen in realistic focus," she pleaded. "He's evaded the matrimonial trap for forty-four years—"

Helen's mascara-caked lashes flew apart. "Good heavens, he's old enough to be your father!"

"Well, yes, if he'd got to it the minute he got his driver's license, I suppose," Maggie agreed. "But this is all old news."

Helen shrugged. "Somehow, holding Annabella close opened up a closed door in my mind, made it all seem so new, worthy of a second look. I know it seems incredible, but . . ." Helen turned the baby on her lap so they were face-to-face. "You are a dolly, aren't you?"

"I'm sure once you calm down, you'll find Owen suitable all over again," Maggie predicted.

"I do so love his company at my parties," Helen admitted. "He'd have been such an asset last night. Had you bothered to come."

"He wouldn't have disrupted his schedule," Maggie pointed out, her mouth twitching with humor. It was well known in social circles that Owen carried his rituals to an amusing extreme.

"But surely if you'd insisted . . ."

"You know better. Last night he had his every-other-Thursday meeting of Relatives of the Revolution."

"He'd have adored that federal aide who recently took the bullet for the President," Helen countered. "He showed your father the wound. If you'd shown up, you could've phoned Owen and given him the choice."

"He never would've veered from his routine."

"You don't—"

"I do, Mother, I do," Maggie broke in firmly, reaching for the diaper bag sitting atop Ryan's tackle box. "I believe you're testing the waters here to see if perhaps Owen can be molded into something new. Trust me, he cannot."

"But—"

"I also think it's about time you handed over Annabella to me. By the smell of things, I'd say she's done more than burp over Owen's attributes."

"Margaret Marie!" Helen cried, wasting not a moment in whisking Annabella down on the square pad laid out by her daughter. "You can't believe there's a real connection."

Maggie sighed deeply as she turned to her mother. "I really don't know what to believe about a lot of things right now."

Helen's face pinched in distaste as Maggie peeled off the baby's miniature jeans. "Do you know how to change a diaper, darling?"

"Yes, Mother, I read all about it in a book."

Helen gasped in genuine awe. "There's research on such things?"

"Thankfully, yes. Please get me the box of wipes."

Helen gratefully moved away from the operation. "How clever to put it all on paper," she gushed. "Now I really must dash, darling, even though I hate to." She hovered over Annabella's squirmy form with a gooey expression. "Your mother must miss you like mad, babycakes. Ta-ta."

Maggie thought about the missing mother as she readjusted Annabella's outfit. She'd already spent considerable time thinking about the woman's plight, wondering just what would drive her to abandon her child. She'd approached this case as she would any other, by attempting to put herself in the place of the key players. The exercise had affected her profoundly! For the first time in her life she'd taken on a mother's perspective, had gone through the motions of giving a hundred percent to a totally dependent creature. It was an exhausting process, but incredibly real and satisfying. She'd never learned so much or cared so much. Not ever!

How extraordinary, to take two people into her life at the same time, who would steer her into brand-new channels of thinking.

She tugged the baby up into a sitting position. Annabella's hazel eyes were hypnotic, her smile as dazzling as the sun itself as she focused on Maggie. She couldn't help but bask in the child's innocent affection for a spell.

Finally, Maggie rose to her knees with a groan. "Okay, baby," she said, "I guess the only game you and

Helen didn't play was telephone. Let's call around and see if we can locate Darla Faye."

WHEN TIMOTHY UNLOCKED Maggie's outer office door at five o'clock that afternoon, he discovered Maggie at Jenna's desk with Annabella standing on tiptoe on her lap. Together they were chatting on the telephone, Maggie in steady professional tones, Annabella in chirpy spurts.

Maggie nodded to him and gestured for him to take the baby. He took off his leather jacket with deliberate care so he could linger over the endearing sight of energetic Annabella, snuggling against Maggie's torso, her fat little fingers entangled in her rippled red mane and the telephone cord and Maggie blowing the babe's russet curls away from her nose as she slowly repeated the terms of someone's will.

He raked a hand through his black, windblown hair, regarding them in wonder. Like the lady in his dreams, this Maggie had a heart after all, a warm one that heated his blood and his desires.

Maggie hung up and carefully untangled the baby from the springy cord.

"You're a natural, Maggie," he observed, edging his lean, hard thigh along the edge of the desk.

She eyes him keenly. "A natural what, Ryan?"

"A natural woman," he crooned, mingling his large fingers with the baby's in her hair.

"You have sex on the brain, Ryan," she complained, shivering as his fingertips grazed her scalp.

"Took you almost twenty-four hours to notice," he noted with a glance at his Timex. "Lucky I'm the detective around here."

It took her almost twenty-four seconds to notice, she silently repeated. But she wasn't in the habit of pursuing every sexual signal she received, especially from earthy types like Timothy Ryan. It had never seemed time-efficient to start relationships that would burn out once the sensual fog cleared.

Would it be any different with Ryan? She eyed him speculatively. He fit the classic bad-boy description, down to his empty pockets and falling-apart clothes. But he wasn't the angry rebel, at war with himself and everybody else. Rather, he strutted around with an inherent good nature, apparently not bothered by his lack of things! A bachelor on the loose without a care. A sexy man who had probably broken dozens of hearts without even realizing it.

She glanced at him as he reached out to tickle the baby. Involvement with him would be risky. But as he scooped Annabella up in the crook of his arm, she was suddenly absolutely certain that he would move heaven and earth to provide for his own family, and allow them to mold him into a more upstanding citizen.

Did she want to be that man tamer?

It was a question that made her redden, and avert her eyes to some paperwork on the desk. It was a question she wasn't ready to to answer. All she knew right now was that she'd missed him again this afternoon, had been anxiously waiting for him to return.

"So, where is Jenna?" he asked, scanning the room.

"She knocks off at five," Maggie replied, sifting through her notes. "She left a few minutes early today. Probably was afraid I'd rope her into some evening baby-sitting if you didn't show up."

His handsome profile grew earnest. "You knew I'd be back, didn't you?"

She beamed. "Certainly, Ryan. I have all your stuff."

"No, no, you know what I mean." He appeared genuinely offended. "I want you to trust me totally and completely. Even when we bicker a bit, I'm committed a hundred percent."

"Yes, I believe you," Maggie admitted. "But Jenna's bound to be a tougher sell, not yet dazzled by your charms."

To her delight, he chuckled. "I can't hope to win over all the girls, I guess."

"A bit of modesty is an appealing quality in a man," she conceded with a shy smile.

"How does supper at the Ryans' pizza place sound?" Timothy asked.

"Your family thinks we're having a thing," she murmured in protest.

"So? Might be just enough to satisfy their curiosity now, so they don't pounce on us unexpectedly. Besides, I'd like to treat you to something for a change."

She toyed with a pencil, avoiding his hopeful gaze. "Look, Ryan, I'm not kidding myself. Guys like you make at least two hundred dollars a day, plus expenses. I'm keeping track of the time you spend on this, minus a small storage fee for cluttering my office and arousing my mother's curiosity."

His brows arched at the mention of her mother. "What did you tell Mama O'Hara?"

Maggie grinned. Helen would pick up a weapon if she heard someone call her mama. "I told her that you're a tenant friend who lost his lease and is working for me."

His jaw sagged and Annabella pushed her fist inside his mouth. "We have a lot to keep straight, don't we?" he said in a garbled voice.

"I figure we each know what works best with our own people," she replied. "We're doing what we have to do."

He closed his eyes as the baby's hand moved up to flick his lashes. "I already told you I don't expect any pay. You're doing a good deed and so am I. So, how about that pizza? Or pasta, if you like?"

Visions of a solitary night in her condo, worrying about Annabella's plight, didn't appeal to Maggie much. "Okay, Ryan. It'll be nice to be around some action."

She gasped in surprise as he suddenly dived to one of the colorful rugs scattered on the hardwood floor with the baby tucked up against him. "What are you doing?"

He lay flat on his back and blinked at her. "Playing, dummy."

Maggie stared down at the pair, who seemed to be involved in a wrestling match. "We need to talk business."

"No, Bella, Bella, no," he protested, rolling back and forth with the baby set on his chest. "Not the triple-blaster belly flop!"

Maggie made an exasperated noise. "C'mon, now!"

"Okay, Maggie," he relented, "you can be the referee. But keep it a fair fight. Tell this kid to stop biting."

Maggie watched in amazement as Annabella sank her tiny white teeth into the tender side of Timothy's forearm.

"Hey, that ain't chocolate, you monkey," he wailed in feigned pain.

Maggie rolled her chair closer to the action. "I couldn't find a trace of Darla Faye," she reported, hoping to get his attention.

"Damn—I mean, darn," he corrected, tweaking Annabella's cheek.

"What do you think that means, Ryan?"

Timothy kept his eyes on the baby, lifted his knees and set her against his thighs, then rocked on his spine. Annabella clutched the soft fabric of his T-shirt and screamed excitedly.

Maggie's fingers curled into fists on her lap. How could he be so charming one minute, then so impossible the next? "Can't we talk while you play?" she asked shrilly.

"Sure," he agreed with an odd gleam. "If you come down here with us."

"Why?" she demanded plaintively.

"Because it's fun."

She eyed the rambunctious pair with misgiving, but ultimately surrendered, and dropped to her knees on the rug. Annabella instantly gave Maggie's hair a sound yank, as though testing her grip. "Okay, let's talk."

"Do you ever stop talking, Maggie?" Timothy said huskily.

She would've been offended if his eyes hadn't been sparkling like the clearest seawater beneath his long black lashes, if his lips weren't quirked suggestively. He wanted to kiss her. No, he was determined to kiss her. And she wanted him to, she realized with a stab of excitement.

But why? He was right, she never did stop talking—or thinking, or questioning, for that matter. This mutual attraction was probably just natural curiosity, a need to discover what it would be like to taste someone so different, someone so maddening.

These thoughts tumbled through her brain as she felt herself being pulled closer and closer to Ryan, with a dizzying anticipation. Amazingly, she couldn't feel his touch anywhere. It was as though she was being drawn by a magnetic force.

Still, he had to be doing it. But how? She lowered her eyes to find both of his hands still clamped to the baby in the cradle of his thighs. It was Annabella who was playing cupid! With a handful of Maggie's hair for a towrope, she was tugging her on a steady course toward Ryan.

The moment his mouth covered hers, Annabella's fingers fell away and Ryan took over completely. His touch was everywhere now, her temple, her throat, the curve of her breast. And all the while he kissed her as she'd never been kissed before—thoroughly, languidly, exquisitely.

Timothy was aware of the fact that Annabella had tumbled out of his lap under her own steam, and he wondered how she could possibly be so clever. He wondered it for a full five seconds before hauling Maggie against him for more intimate contact. Maggie released a low moan as his hand skimmed the curve of her hip over her skirt. Winding a hand around his neck, she lifted herself up higher on his chest to tease and flick his tongue with her own.

The love play went on and on, a sensual fireworks display, full of smaller detonators that exploded with every point of contact. And he'd thought their verbal duels were exciting!

Maggie finally broke free with a spent sigh. "Well."

"Well, well, well," he answered with pleasure.

"So, where's the baby?" Maggie struggled to her feet, straightening her suit, tucking in her blouse. She took a few awkward steps into her inner office, and cried out in alarm.

Timothy was instantly at her side.

"Annabella's into the chocolate again!" she reported over her shoulder, and dropped down to scoop up her candy dish from Annabella's lap. "Oh, baby, how did you know I refilled that? And how did you ever reach it?"

Annabella smacked her tiny legs together on the polished floor, her chocolate-covered face beaming. "Cho-cho."

"You should be trying to say ma-ma," Maggie gently admonished. "I need the towelettes, Ryan," she announced.

Timothy handed her the box from the bookshelf, then sank into a nearby chair. "No leads on Darla, eh?" he asked as he watched the exchange between woman and child. "That's weird."

"Keep your sticky fingers out of my hair," Maggie scolded with a laugh as Annabella reached up to pull the luxuriant red mane falling into her face.

"Business, Maggie, business," Timothy teased.

"I checked everywhere," Maggie turned to tell him. "Telephone and city directories, the postal service, motor vehicles, tax offices, marriage records. Nothing, I—"

Timothy pressed his fingers to her lips as he noticed the doorknob on the outside door jiggling. Maggie followed his gaze through the reception area and sure enough, there was a shadowy figure hovering beyond the frosted glass, testing the lock.

Timothy instinctively put himself in front of the females just as the door popped open.

Maggie tossed the tide of hair away from her flushed freckled face to greet their visitor. "O-O-Owen... Hello." She leapt to her feet and ran out of the inner office.

Timothy managed a sly look at their visitor as he bent down to scoop up the baby.

What a treat Owen Fortescue was close up. He stood at about five foot seven, only a couple of inches taller than Maggie. A pricey dark suit gave him a passable figure, but could not disguise his rail-thin form. His hair was a mixture of wheat and white, cut by a pro who'd mastered the art of disguising a pronounced widow's peak. His pale facial hair was trimmed in a thin slash beneath his beaky nose and a teardrop on his chin. Timothy smirked. A drop-shaped goatee for a class-A drip!

"What is going on here, Maggie?" Owen Fortescue demanded in disbelief.

Maggie deliberately steered him to Jenna's desk, so he didn't have a clear view of her inner sanctum full of Timothy Ryan's belongings. "Just entertaining a client," she answered with a sheepish expression.

"We have many clients at the accounting firm," Owen remarked coolly, "whom it's been my duty to entertain. Never once have I taken off my loafers, or tumbled about the floor to do so."

"Owen, the baby was on the floor and the baby is the client."

"And . . ." he prodded in disdain, his gray eyes shifting to the impressive male figure holding the baby.

"Owen Fortescue, this is Timothy Ryan. He's a private detective who's working for me."

Timothy's tone matched Owen's as he sauntered closer. At an impressive six foot one, he dwarfed the smaller, dapper-looking man. "That outside door was locked, O-O-Owen. We didn't hear you knock."

"I have a key," Owen replied succinctly.

Maggie turned to Timothy apologetically. "I forgot about his key."

"What difference does it make to him?" Owen asked, his face reddening angrily.

Maggie strolled round the room, and cut off the view of Ryan's things with a casual tug to the connecting office door. "Ryan is helping me on a security matter. He's advised me to keep things buttoned up."

"Well, get your things," Fortescue instructed with a eloquent wave. "You can tell me all about it at dinner."

Maggie's hand stole to her kiss-swollen mouth. "Oh, Owen, I forgot about dinner."

"You're awfully forgetful today," Ryan muttered softly.

"That is impossible, Maggie," Owen announced in a strained voice. "We always dine out on Fridays. And this is Friday."

"I am so sorry, but I have a responsibility to this baby."

Owen rocked on his heels for a long moment, weighing the situation. "This is distressing," he said finally, appealing exclusively to Maggie. "I so look forward to our Fridays."

Maggie hesitated indecisively. She'd never had two dates at the same time before. She also couldn't help noting an odd light suddenly dancing in Ryan's dark blue eyes. He was up to something.

"Where were you planning to eat?" Timothy asked pleasantly.

Owen cleared his throat. "Anywhere Maggie likes, of course."

Maggie was nonplussed by the odd question and unbelievable answer. She couldn't imagine Ryan giving up his plans and she couldn't imagine Owen being diverted from his favorite French restaurant on Gloucester Street. She was sent into a deeper state of shock as she watched Owen try to take hold of the baby. Annabella responded with an outraged scream that would have dropped a dog at ten paces.

"We could take the child along, if we must," Owen shouted between gritted teeth.

Maggie fully expected Ryan to snatch the baby right back, and declare that he'd already made arrangements for their threesome. Instead, he moved to his jacket on the green leather chair and reached into the lining pocket, all the while keeping an eye on Owen, who was frozen in place with a mortified look.

"The baby loves to be walked, Fortescue," Ryan confided helpfully. The moment Owen began to pace, Ryan stepped behind him, and held up the enlarged photo of the man in the locket and the Colony Club cocktail napkin in one hand.

Maggie shot him a confused look.

He glared at her, held up the items again, and added another clue by crossing two fingers of the other hand.

Maggie's features brightened. The man in the photo was connected to the exclusive Colony Club! The members-only Colony Club. No wonder Ryan was prepared to let her track down the lead. He probably couldn't think how to get his foot in the door.

"Why don't you go out with Fortescue here," Ryan suggested with an effort. "I'll take care of the baby."

Owen swiveled hard, and dumped Annabella back in Ryan's arms. "How sporting of you, Brian."

"Ryan. The name is Ryan."

"Owen, you have a membership at the Colony Club, don't you?" Maggie inquired sweetly.

"Why, uh, no, I don't," Owen replied with a frown. "It's extremely exclusive. I don't know anyone who belongs."

"But I've always wanted to dine there," Maggie confessed.

He stroked his goatee with pursed lips. "Really? You never mentioned it before."

"With all your connections, surely you can make some arrangement."

"I'm certain they do not serve crayfish mousse, nor your olive-stuffed lamb noisettes," he cautioned.

"I am curious just the same," she insisted. "Call it a whim, if you will."

"You're not particularly whimsical," Owen objected. "And I would like my crayfish."

She fluttered her lashes at Ryan. "Timothy thinks I'm whimsical, don't you?"

It was the first time she'd ever called Timothy Ryan by his given name. He absorbed it like syrup on a pancake. "You're the whimsiest," he replied grandly, and honestly, as he relived their tumble on the floor. If not for the baby, he'd have been tempted to take her—and she'd have let him! The chemistry between them was downright scary!

"Timothy thought perhaps he could get us in to-night—"

"This—this gumshoe?" Owen reared in anger. "I doubt it."

Maggie smiled up at him, smoothing his lapel. "Please try, for me."

"Very well," Owen surrendered huffily. "I'll need a telephone number."

Without thinking, Ryan read the one right off the napkin. He hastily concealed the square under Annabella's shirt when Owen whirled on him in surprise.

"You sure about that, Brian?" he asked sharply. "You behave as though you've been there."

Timothy's blue eyes twinkled as he gave the baby a bounce. "I'm sure, O-O-Owen. I was just about to fulfill Maggie's whim myself when you walked through the door."

"Wouldn't want to be dialing the wrong number," Fortescue muttered as he punched in the numbers.

"The repercussions would be horrific, O-O—"

"Stop calling me O-O-Owen!" he snarled, before sinking into Jenna's chair to address someone on the line.

Maggie shot Timothy a disparaging look, feeling that he had gone too far with his antagonism. But the smug set to his square chin sent back the only message that mattered: his ploy had worked on the upper-crust buffoon. Owen had been tricked into assuming that Ryan had a connection he didn't have. The competitive accountant was bound to move mountains to get into that exclusive club.

Unfortunately an argument ensued with whoever answered the telephone.

"No, I don't have a membership," Owen snapped. "Don't my memberships in five other clubs mean anything?"

Maggie gave Timothy a doubtful frown as the bickering continued.

"Hold on a minute." Owen pressed the mute button on the telephone and turned to Timothy. "You have a connection, big shot. Who is it?"

"No need to be rude, Owen," Maggie objected.

Timothy decided to give Fortescue the line he'd have used, if he had had the prissy manners to blend in and a good suit. "I'd say Adam invited me."

Owen did so. "Adam who? Surely there's only one."

"Cramer," Timothy softly supplied.

"Cramer, that's who!" Owen shouted into the receiver. "I am an accountant for Fiskers and Vale. Everyone knows Fiskers! You do that." He hung on for a few minutes, tapping a pencil in agitation. "Yes? Well, that's better!" He dropped the receiver back in place triumphantly. "Nothing to it! Reservations for eight o'clock."

"Wonderful!" Maggie enthused with a glance at her silver watch. "That leaves us with two spare hours."

"Plenty of time for drinks at a place of my choice," Owen said triumphantly. "Get your coat and purse, Maggie. I'm sure Brian can manage from here on in."

Maggie slipped into her office for her purse and coat while Owen thumbed through his appointment book.

When she returned, Timothy sidled up to her as she eased on her turquoise coat.

"Say goodbye to Maggie, Annabella," he urged, for Owen's benefit.

"Anything else I should know before I go?" Maggie murmured as the baby stroked the shimmery fabric of her coat.

"Annabella and I, well, we want you to know this turquoise color does crazy things to your eyes," he rasped, fingering her collar. "And sets your hair on fire in a man-eating blaze."

She absorbed his boyish, lopsided grin, thinking a decade ago that it probably had all the high school girls' hearts doing somersaults—just as hers was doing now.

She knew better than to fall for a careless man like Ryan, didn't she? Why did he seem so tameable now that she'd kissed him? Why did she have an aching desire to give it a try?

She didn't wish to be married!

Did she?

And even if she did, she wasn't planning to have children.

Admittedly, however, Annabella had awakened her maternal instincts—not to mention her own mother's! But Owen certainly didn't want children, and she'd assumed if she ever walked down the aisle, it would be with him. After all, he was security, with closets full of T-bills and portfolios bursting with stock certificates.

Maggie glanced over at Owen and smiled. He was bent over Jenna's desk, one hand on his appointment book, the other on Jenna's oversized calculator. The machine was spitting out a wave of white register tape as he punched in calculations with sure fingers. A woman most certainly would never be bothered by financial worries with a man like Owen Fortescue. But she'd never really be hot and bothered either, would she? she realized, her smile fading. That seemed to be Timothy Ryan's specialty. She'd been frenzied enough to consummate their brief relationship right there on the floor!

In Owen's defense, however, she'd never given him the chance to fire her up. They'd always kept things simmering below boiling, with lukewarm kisses, and infrequent, restrained sex. Owen liked to keep his body cleansed and his brain focused. Naturally, on occasion, she'd wondered if someone better would come her way. And maybe he finally had....

She suddenly realized that Ryan was looking at her intently as if trying to decipher her thoughts. She drew back a little. "Well, wish me luck."

"I hated to call attention to you with Adam Cramer's name," he murmured with a glance at Owen. "But I don't believe you'd have gotten in without it."

"He's the man in the photo, then," she surmised. "He must be an important Colony Club employee."

"He *is* the club," Timothy corrected tightly. "And he keeps the clientele and club happenings pretty close to the vest."

She released a low whistle. "Sounds like money and muscle."

"Be careful, Maggie," he said hesitantly. "I hope I'm doing the right thing, sending you off this way."

Maggie sensed that he was worried about her trying to crash an old Boston establishment like the Colony, and to her surprise, it made him all the more endearing. "You did everything right, here, Ryan," she said effusively, patting Annabella's russet head. "Thanks."

Timothy watched silently as Owen wedged in between them and linked arms with Maggie. "I'll be back here around midnight," she announced as she stepped into the hallway. "To pick up the baby. Okay?"

Air whistled through Timothy's teeth, as though he were slowly deflating. "Sure. Have a ... have a safe time."

"Of course we'll have a safe time!" Owen said curtly before closing the door on them.

Timothy shifted the baby from one arm to the other with a bleak expression. "She said I did everything right, kid," he murmured, "so shouldn't I have the girl right now? From a female's point of view, what do you think?"

Annabella reached out, clamped her fingers on his nose, and twisted. Hard.

6

"SO LET ME get this straight, Timmy," John Ryan said pointedly an hour later at Ryan's Pizzeria. "Your new girlfriend is out on a date with another man and you are baby-sitting her friend's baby."

Timothy rolled his eyes under his father's relentless questioning. They were standing in the alcove of the family's small no-frills restaurant, the pine reservations podium between them. Timothy wished he had a dollar for every time they'd stood in this same position over the years. His pop had spent most of his adult life in the restaurant, so most of the family dramas were played out here, especially in this alcove.

The place was like a second home to all the Ryans, and decorated like one, with beige Formica tables, church-pew benches, hanging pots full of miles of vines, and huge photographs of the city on the clean plaster walls.

Timothy's cursory peek into the brightly lit dining room confirmed the fact that both his pretty, raven-haired sisters, Kate and Therese, were working the tables with their mother. Both in their thirties with families of their own, they still liked to be a part of things at the restaurant.

"Am I right, or am I wrong?" John pressed unmercifully, raking a hand through his snowy thatch of hair. "Well, boyo?"

To Timothy's relief the phone beside the reservations book rang for the third time in five minutes.

"Ryan's Pizzeria," John murmured into the mouthpiece with a distinctive, silky brogue.

Timothy used the downtime to untie the hood of Annabella's red coat. He pushed it off and her burnished curls instantly sprang to life. "That's better, baby," he murmured, rubbing his nose against hers.

"Don't get too attached to another man's child," John gruffly advised as he dropped the receiver back in its cradle and jotted a name into the open reservations book.

Annabella, finding herself within reach of John's face, made a grab for his bushy white moustache, then babbled in wonder, presumably over the feel of the stiff bristles.

Unable to ignore any baby for any length of time, John reached a beefy arm over the podium to graze the baby's cheek with his knuckle. His expression softened as he studied her sweet, cherubic face. "You bring back a lot of memories," he crooned with a flood of emotion. "You look a lot like our Therese. Ma, come and see this baby!" he called out excitedly. "I swear, she could be a Ryan!"

Timothy flashed him an impudent look. "Mister Indifferent, with the heart of steel."

"Shut up, you," John blustered. "I'm just trying to save your feelings."

A contradiction in terms, but Timothy understood the gist of his message. John Ryan kept his troops in line with plain talk and the old-fashioned work ethic, but he didn't like to see the world take potshots at his own.

Kathleen Ryan bustled forward. Short, plump, with her hair captured in a braided crown, she was approachable in a motherly way and well liked by the patrons.

"Hi, Ma." Timothy beamed affectionately, knowing he could do no wrong with Kathleen. At the sight of him holding a baby who could pass for a Ryan, her light blue eyes glowed with yearning and pleasure.

"Now, there's a perfect fit, if I ever saw one," she greeted him, enveloping the pair in her stout arms. "So where is the young lady lawyer who Patrick says has tamed you so nicely?" She wheeled on her rubber-soled shoes, and gazed toward the restrooms. "Freshening up?"

"Tell your ma where the girlfriend is," John heartily urged, wagging a beefy finger at his son.

Timothy raised a hand in protest. "First of all, Maggie and I are not as cozy as Uncle Patrick has led you to believe."

"Patrick says you have all your belongings stored at her place," Kathleen pointed out, folding her arms under her ample bosom.

"Stored in her office," he hastened to clarify. "She has the space right above mine—"

"She's the tap dancer you complained about?" John broke in slapping his forehead. "Small world, isn't it, Ma?"

"We are friends and she offered the storage space," Timothy explained.

"That six-month lease flew by, didn't it?" Kathleen murmured regretfully.

Timothy normally didn't mind the family's patchwork conversations. They were easy to follow when one was telling the truth. But when a guy was trying to weave in some small white lies, it helped to stick to the point.

"Now it's harvest and you've not improved yourself," John said reprovingly. "Couldn't help hoping you'd be able to pick up the lease yourself, given the rich opportunities in that fancy area. So embarrassing, our own son broken horse and foot."

"I am not bankrupt!" Timothy protested, stepping aside as a young couple entered, seeking a table. Therese breezed up to take care of them, sensing there was a family meeting in progress. "I have my savings," he continued in a lower tone, "which I will not touch until I do settle down—"

"Just come back home if you need a place," Kathleen offered. "Or use the bedroom in back."

"Only if he works the lunch shift," John said. "Mine is one lease that isn't a prize."

Timothy did not have time to work the lunch shift and he didn't want to stray that far from Maggie. Her ritzy leather sofa wasn't such a bad bed.

"So where is your girlfriend?" Kathleen wound back to her original question with the expertise of a gifted weaver.

"He's baby-sitting while she's on a date," John said before picking up the telephone again.

"She's working on a case tonight," Timothy explained to Kathleen, giving Annabella a bounce. "Look, Ma, Maggie O'Hara is really special. Right now, as I said, all we're doing is exchanging favors, the storage space for some baby-sitting and the use of a few Ryan hand-me-downs. It's all new and I can't rush it."

"I think that's nice, and I will make your father think so, too," she promised in a whisper. "Now go back and get something to eat," she directed, holding out her hands to take Annabella. "We'll meet you at table ten, won't we, little one?"

When Timothy arrived at the back table reserved for family with a tray of steaming pasta and a tall glass of milk, it was full of curious family members. His parents had Annabella between them in a high chair, and Kate was tying a bib around her neck.

"I had the cook whip some mild food in the blender for the baby," he told his mother, handing her the bowl. "Thought you might want to do the honors."

"Of course she'd like to do the honors," his father retorted. "With as many bona fide grandchildren as we can collect."

Timothy gave him a wry smile. "Who's at the podium, greeting the customers with the Ryan Irish charm?"

"Therese is taking over the front for a few minutes," John informed him.

Kathleen dipped a spoon into the pasta puree and lifted it to Annabella's open mouth. "People think she is ours, Timmy. How nice it will be when you make that dream come true."

"Can't rush him, Kathleen," John said, drumming his fingers on the tabletop. "After all, he's only twenty-nine. No matter that we had Kate at twenty-two."

Timothy began to shovel spaghetti into his mouth. He was famished and besides he had heard it all before. It wasn't his fault that he'd failed to fall in love. Until now, perhaps. He froze with loaded fork in hand, suddenly finding it difficult to swallow.

Could he really be falling for Maggie in a forever kind of way?

He had trouble believing it possible, with all their differences. Amazingly, even their arguments were stimulating, as though the bickering was some sort of mating dance. And the chemistry between them when they had finally touched . . .

She could feel it too, he was sure. She'd responded in his arms with a deep-seated yearning that cried out for a lifetime of lovemaking.

He gave his raven head an involuntary shake as he took in a mouthful of spaghetti. But could she make the break from O-O-Owen? If that's the kind of man she considered husband material, he was skunked. But she hadn't married him, had she? Just as he hadn't been tempted to marry any of the women he'd dated over the years.

He'd like to think there was a fateful pattern here— his dreams of Maggie and the loss of his lease on the very night that Annabella appeared, which had thrown them together in their mutual need. The theory that their union was planned was an intriguing one. Nuts, but intriguing.

"So what's the plan for tonight, boyo?" John inquired, breaking into his thoughts. "You take care of this child until when?"

Timothy's forehead creased as he fumed over the ongoing interrogation. What a huge price to pay for a simple dinner! "Until Maggie's business meeting is over," he stated with a stiff smile.

Some business. With a flare of jealousy, he wondered if she'd have given Fortescue the brush-off if he hadn't thrown her right into the man's arms. But it was an unexpected opportunity to get inside the Colony Club without too much hassle. Maybe their only chance!

Using Owen Fortescue had been a lazy shortcut, he decided in silent admonishment. All because he felt uncomfortable in those stuffy places. He should've held his ground, insisted she keep their date to come here, suggested they explore the Colony Club tomorrow night as a team. It wasn't like him to back off from a challenge, and it had been niggling at his gut ever since Maggie'd walked out the door on that mousy accountant's arm.

His gaze scanned the table. His family was busy entertaining Annabella with utensils and condiment holders. His dad, in the midst of performing his renowned spoon trick, had the concave end of a utensil plastered to the blunt tip of his nose. That was the final sign, Timothy recognized with a slight shake of his head: Annabella had the gruff old Irishman completely in the palm of her pudgy hand.

"Anybody mind if I cut out for a while?" Timothy asked anxiously. "Ma, you don't mind watching the baby till midnight, do you?"

"I think we can manage," his mother returned in surprise. "But don't you have an obligation to Maggie O'Hara?"

"All Maggie cares about is that Annabella be kept safe and happy."

"Let him go, Kathleen," the old man carefully mumbled around the metal handle dangling over his lips. "By the funny look on his face, I'd say he's off to check out Miss O'Hara's business meeting."

"The funny look on *my* face, Pop?" Timothy eased off the bench, plucked the spoon from his nose and rapped him on the head with it. "See ya around."

Everyone, including Annabella was laughing as he sauntered out of the warm family circle. It was one of those crazy Ryan times that he loved so well. How wonderful that the baby fit right in. And Maggie would too, given half a chance. But first she had to give *him* a chance.

MAGGIE FOUND the Colony Club to be an interesting blend of disparate elements. Located in a Federal town house on Beacon Street overlooking the Boston Garden, it was restored to its original nineteenth-century splendor. The dining room where they'd been seated had a library atmosphere, with polished oak paneling, gilt-framed portraits, and brass chandeliers.

But the patrons weren't the expected bunch of ancient money-mongers that Maggie knew were commonly found in the old respected clubs scattered around the city. There were some notables from politics and industry. Of these, several were with women in their early twenties; others—sworn enemies in public—were apparently meeting together under this neutral roof. And there were the more colorful underworld characters, with suits shiny enough to reflect the sun. Some of them had "dates" too, with troweled-on drugstore makeup.

Maggie absorbed it all, energized with curiosity. This was more than an exclusive club, it was a secret hideaway, a haven with a respectable facade and tight security. Ryan would've fit right in, probably better than she and Owen did. She gave her head a toss in an effort to shake Ryan's image from her mind. This was Owen's time on the meter. He deserved her attention.

When she drew her attention back to her date, seated across the linen-covered table, he was hunched in his carved wooden chair, shaking his head over the wine list. "What a jumbled selection! There are the most impressive vintages of the twentieth century, right down to the most common ones."

"Owen," she leaned forward to whisper. "I believe it's a deliberate attempt to suit the wide spectrum of members."

"So you do recognize the shady characters." He lifted his eyes to Maggie's, his pale brows arched like twin cornstalks. "Had I known this was a hangout for a local thugs, I'd have refused to come."

Maggie's eyes shone with excitement. "Oh, Owen, where is your sense of adventure?"

He gazed around the room at the assortment of paintings and priceless antiques. "Tragic waste of art. Everything is real, you know."

"Respectability, purchased at full retail prices," she agreed with understanding.

Owen wasted no time ordering the steak and potato dinner for both of them, following his longstanding rule that no one could completely destroy a decent cut of sirloin, and that a bottle of full-bodied burgundy would wash away most culinary disasters.

Maggie used the time to peruse the room once again. So this was the lair of Darla Faye's locket companion, Adam Cramer. Who was Darla? Where was Darla? And why was she staying clear of everyone?

There was an aura of danger here that might provoke a woman into action if she feared for her safety or

that of her child. Perhaps Darla was frightened of
Adam Cramer, perhaps she had borne him the child
Annabella, and then made the desperate move to keep
the baby safe by dropping her in Maggie's lap while she
went into hiding on her own. Had Darla set up the late
appointment intending to leave the baby? Or had she
been planning to speak to Maggie, only to change her
mind and flee her office without a word?

Now that she was in the club, with no sign of Darla
Faye or Adam Cramer, Maggie wasn't sure what to do
next. She generally kept to the legal tasks, and hired a
detective to do any necessary spying. Oh, how she
wished that Ryan was here! She'd begun to perceive him
as an appealing partner with different strengths that
complemented hers. But was this fair to Owen? Was she
yearning for Ryan because of his professional skills, or
did she want a dose of his gentle teasing, to bask in the
heat of his sexy gaze?

The blend of professional and personal issues was
new and frustrating.

"Maggie, you haven't touched your salad."

Owen's admonishment snapped Maggie out of her
pensive wonderings. She smiled, examining the salad
plate set before her. "Looks delicious," she enthused,
stirring the dollop of creamy dressing through the
mound of leafy greens.

"It isn't half-bad," he remarked with undisguised
surprise, taking another taste.

And Owen wasn't half-bad in a lot of ways, Maggie
reminded herself. He'd always shown her respect along
with restrained affection. And it had always seemed
enough. At the very least, he deserved the chance to
shine as Ryan did. After all, he didn't know she had new

emotional needs, or how appealing she found Ryan, with his easygoing style and simple tastes. Perhaps Owen could be fun, too.

"Uh, Owen?" she ventured, her eyes sparkling over the flaming amber candle holder.

He held up a hand as he munched his lettuce with precise chews, then swallowed. "Yes, dear? Go on."

She took a long sip of ice water. "I have something to ask you."

"By all means." He set down his fork and fixed her with penetrating gray eyes.

"What do you think of my coat?"

He blinked absently. "What coat, Maggie?"

"The one I'm wearing tonight," she clarified lamely, realizing by his tone that he'd expected an earthshaking query.

He drew his lips together in a wry pucker. "You really want to know?"

"Yes, Owen, really," she assured him sweetly. "I've had it for a few months now, and you've never commented on it."

He studied the garment draped over her high-backed chair. "I think it is unsuitable for chilly autumn weather," he declared with a heavy sigh. "I can see it as a spring cover-up, but it's too flimsy for these unpredictable nights. Wear your gray wool next time, I should think."

"About the color," she coaxed. "Does it suit me?"

"In your role as an attorney, I think not," he confided with a measure of regret. "We are always honest with each other, Maggie, and I think a bright blue-green shade sends out, well, unusual, flagrant signals."

"The color is turquoise!"

"Hmm, yes," he agreed dryly. "The glossiest example I've ever encountered."

"Some might call it a crazy sparkle," she prompted, fluttering her lashes to bring attention to her green eyes. Surely he could see anything Ryan could see, given a fair chance and a shove in the right direction.

He gave her a faintly condescending smile. "There's a fine image for the courtroom."

"Owen, I want you to try to eliminate the professional angle from your judgment. On a strictly personal level, how does the color suit me?" Maggie pulled the fabric over her shoulder and drew the collar beneath her hair and close to her eyes. She inhaled nervously. Tension cut the air like a knife.

"I really don't know what to say," he faltered with a short, self-conscious laugh. "This whole conversation seems pointless."

Maggie reached across the table and grabbed his wrist. "Answer me!"

His gray eyes bulged in surprise. "All right," he huffed. "Any shade of green clashes with your hair—"

"What!" She snatched her hand back in disgust.

His mouth sagged in confusion. "You asked me, remember? Isn't that what you want to know?"

"But my eyes are green!" she cried. "Do they clash with my red hair?"

"Maggie, I can't say I study your eyes much," he offered in excuse. "But don't worry, they're not bright enough to clash with your hair—"

"Not bright enough?" she repeated in disbelief.

"It isn't like you to moon over the inconsequential," he chastised her impatiently. "If you are looking for my approval of your taste in clothes, I'm afraid I cannot give it. I long ago made a vow to accept your choices without complaint."

"How noble," she said tightly.

"You have only yourself to blame for this distress," he insisted disdainfully. "You were looking for fashion advice, and I gave it!"

"Believe me, Owen, all in all, I got exactly what I was looking for."

"Then you will take my words to heart and review your wardrobe."

Maggie shook her head in resignation. Owen was only behaving in character. Didn't he realize that the generous thing to do would've been to give her a nice compliment and carry on? Instead, he had viewed it as a chance to release some criticism that had undoubtedly been festering inside him for a long time. How many other things about her had he been tolerating? Ever since she'd known him she'd foolishly considered herself exempt from his contempt. She should've tested these waters a long time ago.

Their wine and food arrived soon after and their conversation reverted to the sophisticated exchanges their relationship was built upon. Owen attempted to reestablish their regular level of camaraderie, but it was too late.

One taste of Timothy Ryan had left her the hungriest woman on earth.

One taste of Timothy Ryan, and she couldn't help but view her relationship with Owen as a disappointing half-empty glass, rather than the satisfactory half-full one she'd once believed it to be. Never having experienced the raw electricity of a man until now, she'd assumed that it was pure fantasy, the stuff of fiction.

For the first time ever, Maggie's sexual appetites were burning a hole in the pit of her belly. She'd had a couple of intimate encounters in college, but they were relationships of the times, immature choices based on youthful curiosity and peer pressure. Maggie wanted Ryan in her bed like she'd never, ever wanted a man. She longed for him to whisper sweet compliments in her ear, and to nibble that ear, too. They would laugh in bed. She knew it.

She sipped the musty wine, aware that it was tart, a clear extension of the man who had chosen it. She twirled the stem of her glass in her fingers, returning Owen's perfunctory smile with a weak one.

"Owen, I . . ." She trailed off, staring at a rather nice copy of Boilly's *The Movings*. The picture of several families on a Paris street, in transit with all their possessions, was rather symbolic. "I want to move on."

Owen sliced a wedge of steak, his eyes never leaving his plate. "I do, too. This club is not for us. But you just needed to be shown, didn't you?"

"You misunderstand. I'm not interested in exclusivity anymore," she explained. "In our relationship."

That bombshell drew his full attention! The meat never made it to his mouth. "You are overwrought, that's all. You need a good night's sleep—or something!"

Maggie held his gaze with a clarity she normally saved for the courtroom. "I feel the need to change direction."

His forehead puckered with suspicion. "Seems sudden."

She nodded vigorously. "It's as though a door has magically opened in my mind, allowing a sunbeam to pour through, to cast everything in a totally different light."

His brows arched in speculation. "And this light is shining over me as well, I suppose?"

"In a way," she slowly replied. "It's illuminated what we have together, and what we don't. For instance, Owen, I'm not sure I want to remain childless."

"But you were sure! Sure, right along with me, for two whole years!"

"I'd never been exposed to a baby before Annabella," Maggie explained softly. "I've found that I enjoy caring for her. A lot."

"But surely it's a lark, something that will pass." He nodded sagely, and returned to his food.

"I don't think so."

"It's my guess you haven't had much rest since you took on the baby," he said with a superior smile. "You are suffering from sleep deprivation."

She made a disgusted sound and pounded on the table. "I am trying to be honest with you, Owen."

"I'm sure you are," he granted, reaching for his wineglass. "The fog will clear and you'll be all right again. I guarantee it."

Maggie studied him with sympathy and annoyance. He was so removed from real emotion that he considered her desire for a child something that would "pass." But Maggie had never seen things so clearly. And it all seemed due to a two-bit private eye and a child whose only utterance was "cho-cho." Impossible, but true!

It was during their dessert of cheesecake and coffee that Maggie spotted a man that could be Timothy Ryan's twin brother, right down to the rumpled brown suit. He was standing near the front entrance off the lounge, speaking to the burly bouncer who masqueraded as a maître d'. When he turned to expose his profile, she realized that it was the one and only Timothy Ryan.

Her heart gave a jerky flutter, like the wings of a baby bird. He'd come for her, come because they were an inseparable team. She didn't know whether to hug him for his insight, or bop him for having so little faith in her abilities. But she was going to love mulling over the choices.

7

"MUSCLE-BOUND IDIOT." Owen Fortescue bristled as the maître d' escorted Timothy Ryan through the maze of tables in the dimly lit room. Ryan's brown wool suit was a disaster by Savile Row standards, but he wore it well, well enough to make women's heads turn as he moved through the room.

"There are different kinds of smart, Owen," Maggie returned defensively.

Owen's eyes narrowed to slits, and he raised his voice as Timothy closed in. "I've never seen a finer example of the obvious in my entire life."

"I'm sure there's a compliment tucked away in that comment, O-O," Ryan greeted. He tipped his nearly empty beer glass at his burly, bald-headed escort. "Thanks for the escort, Jeeves. I'll seat myself."

"This man claims to be with your party," the maître d' told the diners in an accusatory tone.

"Three bugs in a rug," Timothy insisted with an imperious air, and sank into the spare chair at the small square table.

"You have a terrible sense of direction," the employee returned suspiciously. "I pointed you toward the dining room ten minutes ago and you ended up in the lounge."

"The lounge is open, isn't it?" Ryan queried, feigning confusion.

"Members, of course, are free to roam. But you, sir, are the guest of a guest."

Ryan sighed in regret. "Ah, but this place has such a homey feel, I just instantly felt at home."

The man's mouth curled in a strained smile. "I am assuming you won't need a menu."

Timothy looked at the cheesecake and coffee Maggie and Owen were having. "Guess I'm a little late for an entrée. But I will have a slice of this cake."

The maître d' cast him a withering look. "I'll tell your waiter."

"A little more fudge on top, if you don't mind," Timothy called after the retreating employee.

"Don't push it," Maggie advised in a hushed voice, but her green eyes were dancing with delight.

He'd come, and that was all that really mattered.

Owen fingered his moustache as though trying to sculpt his thin lips into a smile. "So, Ryan, are you here on a whim too?"

Timothy was busily pouring coffee from the table's silver decanter into Maggie's white, gold-edged cup. He took a sip from it with an appreciative noise. "Good coffee, good coffee."

"How rude to drink from her china," Owen snorted.

"It's all right." Ryan leaned forward to confide, man-to-man. "I'm here on her whim."

Lost in the verbal sparring match, Owen sought distance by leaning back in his chair. Maggie knew it was gibberish to him. Owen's conversation was always reasoned and objective. And in all fairness, their upper-class circle loved him for it, including her own parents, who could always depend upon him to round off a dinner party with up-to-date news from around the world, sort of like a broadcast from CNN. Maggie imagined that Ryan's conversation at her parents' dinner table might be more like a stand-up comedy routine. But again, Maggie had the feeling that a bit of whimsy in her life—or her parents'—wouldn't be such a terrible thing.

"I know I'm supposed to be baby-sitting," Timothy turned to tell Maggie, "but I had some ideas, so I left the baby with my folks."

"Ideas?" Owen repeated, struggling to keep a rein on his temper. "What is he doing here, Maggie? More to the point, what are we all doing here?"

"Isn't that a little philosophical for a Friday night on the town, O-O-Owen?" Timothy asked, straightening up as his dessert came.

"I am ready for the check," Owen told the waiter abruptly.

Timothy dug into the cake with gusto. "I mean, those sort of brain-busting questions are better left for a sunny day over on the Common, lyin' flat on your back on a blanket of autumn leaves. Wouldn't you agree, Maggie?"

Maggie's lovely eyes widened as the pair sandwiched her with expectant looks. Seeing herself lying on a blanket of leaves in the park across from her office was an enticing image. It was the kind of thing only Timothy Ryan would dare ask her to do. She couldn't imagine Owen flat on his back in public unless he'd slipped on an icy sidewalk.

She closed her eyes to conceal the amorous gleam that was bound to be shining in her gaze. The picture was growing more vivid in her mind—their bodies pressed together, crunching leaves, the cool ground.

She took several breaths in an effort to steady her pulse. "I think you misunderstand Owen's question, Timothy," she finally suggested gently.

"He knows exactly what I mean," Owen snapped shrilly.

"It's your call, Maggie," Timothy said with a deferential wave.

"This is all about a case," she explained quietly.

Owen's straw-colored head bobbed. "I think I'm beginning to see. You used me to gain entrée to this seedy club."

"You seemed just the man to get us in," Timothy replied, handing Maggie back her cup.

Maggie set it back in her saucer, not daring to sip from it under Owen's explosive look. "Owen, you insisted we dine out tonight," she said calmly. "I am on a stiff schedule and could see no harm in checking out this place during our date."

"Date?" Owen bit back. "You call this threesome of ours a date?"

"No, Owen," she reasoned with strained patience. "I didn't know Ryan was going to show up—"

"Don't you think I saw how you were going to put your mouth on that cup just now, after—after him?" Owen sputtered. "Surely you don't take me for an utter moron."

Timothy's deep masculine chuckle rippled through the electrified air. "You put it so well, Fortescue, when you said 'I've never seen a finer example of the obvious in my entire life.'"

Owen made a disgusted noise. "I can hardly believe it, but it's this idiot who's put those ideas about dating others into your head, isn't it?"

"Maggie!" Timothy crowed admiringly. "Spitfire move."

"Shut up, Ryan," she ordered through gritted teeth, as her thighs melted together under his heated gaze.

Owen inhaled deeply, summoning patience. "Maggie, you're not yourself right now. This case has taken its toll on you, somehow. Be smart and leave with me now. We'll have a quiet drink at your place, relax, and put this entire episode, including your coat, behind us."

Timothy brightened over the mention of the coat. "Does crazy things to her eyes, doesn't it?" he raved, skimming her chin with his finger. "Blazing green and blue in a big fireworks display."

Owen scowled as Maggie basked in his attention. "So you're responsible for her childish ramblings—about inconsequential colors, about doors of light!"

"Owen, I never meant this conversation to go so far in public," Maggie said apologetically but firmly. "But I am serious about my wish for more freedom."

"But I thought we had an understanding—"

"You give her a ring?" Timothy broke in to ask.

"Well, no," Fortescue blurted back. "But two years—"

"Two years of what?" Ryan squawked, his heart slamming with energy. He'd hoped he might have the chance to stake some kind of claim eventually, and this was made to order. This bozo had been stringing her along forever, probably on nothing but a few vague feelings and some pricey dinners. It was his pleasure to force her into a reality check.

"We've had a satisfying arrangement," Owen returned blisteringly. "One which is none of your business. Not all men just grab what they want! With big paws and four-syllable sentences."

"I say you've taken exactly what you want," Ryan countered, a crafty gleam in his eye. "With stealthy, shoplifter fingers and seven-syllable bullshit that adds up to zero in the commitment department."

Owen's mouth curled in a snarl. "Think you're pretty smart, don't you?"

Timothy's smile didn't quite reach his eyes. "I have my moments."

"Enough!" Maggie interrupted tersely. "This isn't the time or the place for this discussion."

"Finally, something we agree upon." Owen stood up, dropping his napkin on his half-eaten dessert. He reached into his jacket for his wallet and extracted a couple of bills. "Here is my share of the check, Maggie. Since you're so intent on freedom, I'm sure you'll want to handle your share."

"All right, Owen," she agreed with a small nod.

He took a step, then turned for one last attempt. "You will come to your senses, I'm certain of it."

"I'll contact you immediately if that happens," Maggie promised, delicately dabbing her mouth with her napkin.

"Don't do so unless this fullback is gone for good. Understand?"

"Understood," she murmured.

"What a sore loser," Timothy noted as Owen stormed out of the dining room.

"Not sore enough," Maggie said, bowing her head self-consciously. "He walked away wondering just how long it will take me to get over my insanity."

His eyes lit up tenderly. "You can lock me away in your asylum anytime, baby."

Her eyes twinkled. "Very funny."

"Just an obvious attempt to break the ice with the ridiculous."

"That rumpled suit of yours makes any other attempts unnecessary, Ryan," she assured him.

He gave her hand a squeeze. "Now wouldn't you be rumpled if you'd been folded away in a box in your office?"

Caught between two men and a baby, Maggie did feel rumpled and out of sorts! But she wouldn't give him the satisfaction of knowing that. He'd had his quota of fun for the evening. Not that that pompous jerk Owen didn't deserve it.

"I hope you didn't feel pressured by me to make that major move at the end," Timothy ventured quietly, studying his fingernails.

Her eyes flashed emerald fire. "The hell you hope that!"

He raised his hands in surrender. "Okay, so I wanted Owen to slither away. I'm a selfish keowt, a contemptible fellow."

"Well, you don't have to look so smug about it," she complained with a grudging grin. "Takes almost all the sincerity out of your confession."

"I'd never want to hurt you, Maggie, you know that, don't you? I just want a chance with you." To his delight, she curled her fingers around their mutual cup and took a drink.

Maggie sipped slowly, regarding him with a gemstone stare. Already he was saying things that Owen never had. Of course she wanted to encourage him, but she was smart too. She had no way of knowing the depth of his feelings for her. And it would take a while to find out. But her feminine intuition told her the discovery would be worth tonight's trouble.

"So, now what?" she asked softly.

"We eat our cheesecake and wait," he replied. "I think I've stirred up enough trouble in the lounge to get Adam Cramer's attention."

Timothy's theory was soon confirmed when their small, wiry waiter, who should've been set to give them the bum's rush, suddenly appeared at the table with a fresh carafe of coffee and an extra cup for Ryan.

"O-O-Owen either slipped this guy a hefty tip or I'm on the right track," Timothy muttered under his breath.

"Owen might have slipped him his parking stub for validation, but nothing more that." Maggie leaned closer with real interest. "So just where are we going on this track of yours?"

He moved his raven head close to her burnished red one. "Well, I got to thinking about the check you did on Darla," he whispered, "and the way it turned up empty. That just seemed strange. Everybody leaves traces. And I'm sure her trouble is new, at least as recent as Annabella. So why wouldn't there be any listings for her?"

Maggie's creamy forehead wrinkled in thought. "Because Darla Faye isn't her real name?"

"Right."

"But it's such a jazzy name. Not one to hide behind."

"Exactly! And what do you find in nightclubs? In lounges?"

"Entertainers!" she whispered in triumph. "Yes, Ryan, that's a stage name if I ever heard one. And her voice was smooth on the telephone, despite the fact that she had a hard-edged attitude. She could very well be a singer."

"With that hunch to go on," he continued, "I hung around the bar for a couple of beers, and studied the easel near the entrance where the entertainers' pictures are displayed."

"Any mention of her?"

"Nothing. The bartender was keeping a close eye on me, being a non-member and all, so I decided to run a bluff on him. I said I'd heard Darla Faye perform and wondered when she'd be back."

"What did he do?"

"Went white as a sheet." Timothy smiled proudly over the memory. "He was on the phone the minute he pushed another beer on me. You know, those beers didn't cost me a nickel. Funny how good things come to those who deserve them."

Maggie mulled things over with a sip of coffee. "I hope this was wise, showing our hand this way."

Timothy shrugged. "It might have been smarter to speak to Darla first, but she's made that very difficult. And the chance to get in here presented itself so suddenly." He paused as though on the brink of a heart-wrenching confession. "I might have had a tough time getting us in here without Owen."

Maggie's lush red mouth curved endearingly. "You wouldn't have gotten us in here on a bet."

Timothy was unoffended. "So then we'll just forge ahead, confident that this was the only route to take."

"The only tree to shake," she laughed in agreement.

"I love this going-steady stuff."

As she gasped in surprise, he reached for her wrist and kissed her tender pulse point.

They were so enamored with each other, they didn't spot the man approaching their table until his spicy cologne filled their nostrils.

"Good evening," he greeted them silkily. "I am Adam Cramer, your host."

Maggie's heart jumped as she looked up at the distinguished-looking man with a crest of salt-and-pepper hair and chiseled Mediterranean features.

Timothy gave Maggie's wrist a gentle squeeze, then released it to shake Cramer's hand. "Good evening, Mr. Cramer," he said. "Pull up a chair, please."

Maggie felt a wave of admiration for her new partner. He'd set the tone by giving the first directive. Cramer obliged, unbuttoning the jacket of his thousand-dollar pinstripe as he sank into the chair vacated by Owen. But from the severe expression on his narrow, tanned face, it was obvious that deference wasn't a habit.

"Such interesting guests," he observed smoothly with a faint accent, inspecting them both with his dark, penetrating eyes.

"Such an interesting host," Maggie returned evenly. "I've spent a lifetime in Boston and never knew of this club."

He flashed a row of pristine capped teeth. "Ah, but young ladies from Beacon Hill certainly move in different circles, do they not, Ms. O'Hara?"

Maggie was nonplussed by the fact that he'd taken immediate steps to find out exactly who she was, but managed to keep her poker-faced trial demeanor in place. "I don't know, Mr. Cramer," she replied airily. "The retired Justice Emory Steeplehouse was here a short time ago with one of my sorority sisters. But I imagine it's tough for his wife to move around much since her hip replacement last month."

His chuckle was deep and tinged with unmistakable respect. "Local businessmen like Owen Fortescue sometimes crash my place out of curiosity. I humor them, when they are harmless types like him who have heard my name and want to act the big shot."

"Yes," Maggie said with a laugh. "You caught Owen in the act."

Cramer leaned forward on the table, and caught her gaze across the flickering candle with seductive, glittering eyes. "But the plot thickens, does it not? Your private-eye friend here shows up and starts asking questions about Darla Faye."

"Harmless curiosity," Timothy inserted. His voice was calm, but his body had stiffened. Not only had the club owner uncovered Maggie's indentity with swiftness, but his own as well.

Cramer was currently regarding him with cool calculation. "You are not harmless, Ryan, any more than I am. But I am an amiable host at all times." He removed the check from the table and spilled Owen's bills into Timothy's hand. "Your money's no good here tonight."

"This could quickly become my favorite club," Timothy quipped, pocketing the cash.

Cramer's long brows joined over his nose. "I'm interested in a trade off. I want to know what your connection is to Darla Faye."

"We heard her sing not too long ago," Maggie replied easily.

"You've never been here before," Cramer pointed out suspiciously.

"It was a private party," Timothy improvised. "One of those crazy, spontaneous things that happen when a piano's in the room."

Cramer's heavy brows rose. "Really? What is your favorite part of her act?"

"She does a hellava sweet version of 'Witchcraft,'" Ryan answered with convincing admiration.

Cramer stroked his jaw thoughtfully. "What if I told you that she's a magician?"

"Then we'd say you're not paying much attention," Ryan bantered back.

Maggie swallowed hard. Ryan took a chance at every turn. With her, with Owen, with strangers like Cramer. It was such a different way to live. Could she stand it? Would she have a heart attack before her next birthday? Before the night was through?

Cramer waved a slender hand. "All right. Maybe you're on the level. I want you to understand, however, that my suspicion is justified. Darla Faye is missing. That's why the bartender alerted me to your query, Mr. Ryan."

"Poor Darla," Maggie instantly murmured apologetically.

Cramer's face furrowed in concern. "Do you know anything that might be of help to me, Ms. O'Hara?"

"Not really."

"I don't understand." Cramer's voice had a sharper edge. "You've never heard of this place, then you show up here to speak to Darla, shortly after she's gone missing."

Maggie's lovely features were a guileless mask. "Oh, didn't I mention the locket with your picture in it?" Both men gave her shocked looks, but she continued to regard Cramer innocently. "That night at the party, Darla insisted I try it on. And wouldn't you know, I accidentally ended up keeping it! I can't tell you how surprised I was, to come here in search of her, only to find out her boyfriend runs this place!"

Adam Cramer chuckled right along with her. "I am a happily married man, Ms. O'Hara. Darla is a happily single employee. If my picture is in her locket, I assure you, it's because of the business friendship we share."

"Oh, if you say so," Maggie agreed with a dismissive wave.

"I would like to have that necklace, please." Adam Cramer's smile had thinned to an angry slit as he reached a hand across the table.

Maggie rummaged through her purse as though trying to oblige. "Let me see here—" She gasped as Cramer snatched the bag to search for himself.

"Try and understand how concerned I am for Darla's safety," he said over her murmurs of protest. He nearly tossed the purse back at her when he came up empty-handed.

Maggie's eyes grew wide in apprehension. "Oh, Timothy, what if I've lost it? After all the trouble we went to to locate the owner."

Timothy didn't miss a beat. "That was incredibly stupid," he told her harshly. "We'll have to try and replace it now. I hope it isn't too valuable, Cramer," he said in a sympathetic tone. "If Darla turns up, tell her we're looking for her. That we'll make it up to her somehow." Timothy rose from his chair to shake hands with their fuming host.

"What's the hurry?" Cramer said abruptly in an effort to stall them. "Stop by the lounge, for a last drink on the house."

"Certainly the kind of freebie hospitality you like best," Maggie complained to her partner, fueling the smoke screen for a swift escape.

"I've had enough fun for tonight," Timothy shot back with a haughty look.

"Cheapo here is just mad because he'll have to chip in on the necklace," she said shrilly to Cramer.

"I will not!" Timothy exclaimed indignantly, deftly easing Maggie's coat over her shoulders. "You lost it, you replace it!"

"If you felt that way, you shouldn't have driven Owen away!" she cried out, forcing her lower lip to tremble. She glanced at Cramer, relieved to see he appeared very interested in their little melodrama.

"I thought maybe there was the chance to hear Darla again—" Timothy cut himself off in fury. "Oh, never mind. This was all a mistake!"

"All men are a mistake," she hissed back, and cast Cramer an apologetic look over her shoulder as Timothy steered her toward the alcove.

Adam Cramer grasped her arm as they neared the door. "Ms. O'Hara, has it occurred to you that you brought some of this trouble on yourself?"

Maggie swallowed, not daring to look at Timothy. Was she a sigh away from being caught in her lie? If Cramer had seen through their staged argument, and had decided to have his hovering maître d' tip her over like a bottle of ketchup, the first thing to drop into view, would be Darla's locket, now wedged snugly in the confines of her see-through bra.

"What I mean to say," Cramer continued, "is that this creative dating scheme of yours is a bit strange and unseemly."

"Somehow, I felt right at home here with our trio," she replied saucily with a wink. "Good night."

"We did it!" she enthused as they trotted around the side of the building to the club's parking lot.

"That's a closer shave than I like," Timothy confessed, guiding her toward his old Impala.

Maggie paused beside the passenger door, her face beaming in the moonlight. "Who are you trying to kid? You live for shaves like that."

"Yeah, yeah. But I'm a solo act, remember? Worrying about you took a year's growth off me. Telling him about the locket was risky."

"I know it," she admitted, her fingers stealing to the chain. "Especially since I had it right here all along."

"I know that! Spotted the chain hours ago in your office," he scoffed. "That fancy bra of yours draws the eye. Gives a guy ideas."

"Really? What sort of ideas?"

"Lots of neat ideas," he answered with a leer. "But that doesn't excuse your decision to bait the man."

"I couldn't bear to leave that place without finding out where he stands," she countered.

"You sure managed that. If Darla's in trouble, he's in it all the way."

"Admit I was wonderful," she prodded with a proud lift of her chin. "Right down to the razzle-dazzle fight scene."

"I'd rate you believably argumentative, and say you raised maligning to an art form." His sensuous mouth curved slightly in the shadows as he unlocked her door. "Not bad for an amateur. Thank god Owen took a powder when he did, though. He probably would've babbled us right into concrete Jockey shorts. Panties for you, of course," he added as an afterthought. "One thing I'm sure of, Adam Cramer wouldn't spare anybody, no matter how cute."

"His feelings for Darla prove that," Maggie agreed, easing into the car. "He was about to explode with hostility—over whatever happened."

Timothy closed her door, then rounded the car and climbed into the driver's seat. "That's no regular country club," he stated, staring back at the stately building as he started the engine. "Half the guys in there had records."

"And the other half deserved them," she concurred.

Timothy wasted no time barreling off the property and into the neighborhood's tangle of streets.

"You know, you're really good," Maggie said suddenly, twisting on the seat to study his sturdy profile.

He eased up for a red light, and gave her a pleased smile. "I'd like to think so."

"I mean, following that bluff through about Darla being a singer rather than a magician. Would you call that investigator's instinct?"

He released a thoughtful breath. "Revealing my feelings for you, anticipating that you might return them...that, Maggie, was instinct." He noticed she was flushing nicely, but kept his eyes on the road as the light turned green. "The bit with Darla was mostly deduction. You mentioned that she had the voice for it. And the lounge itself, with its dance floor and speakers, is set up for music. I'm sure you'll agree that the Colony Club crowd isn't the type to watch a rabbit jump out of a hat. They want an excuse to haul each other around and rub bodies. Slow dancing to some moody tunes would be just right."

"Pull their own tricks out of the hat," she joked.

His mouth twitched. "You're a quick learner."

They drove along quietly for a few blocks when suddenly their easy silence was interrupted by a pronounced bump and wobble on the driver's side in back. Timothy swore under his breath and steered for the curb.

"Sit tight a minute," he directed as he came to a stop. He left the engine running and climbed out for a look.

Maggie knew there was trouble when he reached in and shut off the ignition. "Flat tire?"

"Yup."

"Guess we're the ones who could use a magician right now," she said, staring anxiously out the windshield.

"I'd settle for a spare tire and a jack. Think positive while I check the trunk."

Her mouth sagged as she turned his way. "You don't even know—"

"I moved, remember," he pointed out defensively, closing the door with a thump.

"Moved from your office to your car to my office!" Her voice bounced off the Impala's white interior, never reaching his ears. How utterly irresponsible of him! She was just about to storm back to the trunk when she heard the recognizable sounds of a clanking jack and bouncing tire. A little ashamed of her quick temper, she cracked open her window to offer help, but he declined. Before long, they were on their way again.

"I suppose that happens a lot with this beater," she speculated on a hopeful note.

He gave her a sobering look. "Not really. My cousin has a tire store in Charlestown, so I get the best tires for the best price."

"So that means the flat was an act of vandalism?"

"A deliberate stall."

"But why, Ryan?"

Timothy pressed down the accelerator. "That's what we're going to find out."

8

"HEY! My stuff!"

"Hey, my whole business!"

Maggie's office was a shambles. Chairs and cabinets were overturned, papers were strewn everyplace. Timothy was furious, but had the foresight to grasp the collar of Maggie's coat to prevent her from charging ahead on her own.

"Let me go!" she yipped. "Whoever it is is long gone."

"Nobody could possibly be long gone," he hissed in her ear. "They didn't have much of a head start." He felt her body go limp under the flowing coat, so he released her. The only weapon in sight was a long crystal vase, tossed on its side on the green leather sofa. He curled his fingers around it and quietly proceeded to the inner office.

"Told you it was empty," Maggie declared in a clear voice, only a step behind him.

He spun on his heel, his expression filled with disbelief. "Don't you ever obey?"

"It's a word that will be taken out of my wedding vows," she confided. "If I ever marry, that is."

Releasing a weary breath, he set the vase down on her cluttered desk. "After tonight, I figure you could wear out one man a week."

"Owen lasted a couple of years," she tossed back as she gave the ransacked room a sweeping inspection.

"Owen never lit your fuse, firecracker."

She wheeled swiftly back on him, to find that his expression was as provocative as his husky tone. She marveled at the effect he had on her. The burning tingle that traveled up her spine was unexplainable magic. He could light her fire with a look and a word.

How sad that she hadn't known, until now, that she could be set aflame this way. How incredible that she was taking the time to notice. Her whole place was a dump, and she was thinking wild and crazy erotic thoughts.

"What are we gonna do?" She sounded tired, drained of her usual energy.

He closed the space between them and cupped her face in his hands. "I think you should call 911, Maggie. Direct them to your condo—"

"No!" she objected. "They'll want answers. They'll want Annabella."

"Do you want your personal belongings pawed through this way?" he challenged, gesturing to his own trashed possessions.

"There are traces of her everywhere at the condo, Ryan. Besides," she added with a pout, "I thought private eyes were always battling the cops."

"That's dumb movie stuff," he snapped impatiently, picking up the receiver of her telephone to see if it still worked. Thankfully, a dial tone buzzed in his ear. He presented her with the receiver and rolled her leather chair up to the desk. She sank down and punched in seven numbers.

He hovered overhead, scratching his chin. "I don't remember 911 being expanded to seven digits."

"Hello, Mort? Yes, this is Maggie O'Hara... Oh, you have ... hang on a second." She pushed the mute button on her console, then tipped her gaze to Timothy. "It's the condo security chief. He's been trying to call here. A couple of young goons with pony tails tried to crash my building."

"Told you, Mag—"

"He stopped them, with a couple of beefy staff and some electronic gizmos. The place makes Fort Knox look like a beach shack."

"The police, Maggie, the pol—"

She rapped the receiver against his flat belly to shush him, then released the mute button. "You did beautifully, Mort. You didn't bother with the police, did you? You did what?" she shrieked. "My father? You called my father?"

Timothy grinned fiendishly over the irritation on her cute little face. Modern woman up against the old boys' network. The boys were bound to be in big trouble.

"I've told you before not to do that, Mort. I know Father's name is on the lease, but that is a legal idiocy concerning my trust fund. Something my grandfather concocted! No, he is not picking up the tab for my place. The trust fund money is my money. When I reach thirty, all will be transferred to my name. No, I don't want you to call the police yet. Just zap anyone who tries to break in with a thousand volts!" She sighed, sagging in her chair. "Yes, of course, if it gets that bad, you'll have to call them. No, I'm not sure if I'm coming home tonight. 'Bye." She replaced the receiver with a slam.

Timothy's dark blue eyes glinted with mischief. "Seems I'm not the only one with folks who can't mind their own business."

"You certainly are not!" she agreed heartily, punching in a second number. "Hello, Dad?" She held the receiver away from her ear as a baritone barrage flooded the wire. "Dad, listen. I don't want to hear it all again. Leaving the Cambridge firm was not a mistake. I was not necessarily safer. There's trouble everywhere. Besides, I have a capable new detective working for me." She worked her index finger through the phone cord, not daring to look at Ryan as she spoke of him in a complimentary way. "He's taking good care of things. . . . I know Mother liked the baby. No, Dad, she really isn't mine, no matter what Mother says. I don't care if Annabella looks a lot like I did! And I wish you'd tell the condo board of directors that the place is mine, free and clear. I'm tired of Mort and the others acting like dorm mothers. I'll be in touch soon, I promise. I'm perfectly safe. Yes, I promise. Good night, Dad."

She leaned forward, propped her elbows on her cluttered desk and massaged her temples.

"That's not where the real tightness is," he murmured.

Maggie started as Timothy's fingers plunged into her stiff shoulder muscles and he began to knead them with a strong, sure touch.

"Just lose yourself in the motion, Maggie," he coaxed.

Her head lolled back as his fingers edged under her suit jacket. If only they could forget about the case for a while . . . But they had work to do. "We have to talk, you know."

He chuckled deeply. "I guess you're right."

"Why do you suppose Adam Cramer took such drastic measures after letting us go? He had us right there."

Timothy released a thoughtful breath. "I don't think he likes trouble in that little club of his. Customers see trouble, and they think it might spread. They obviously trust that Cramer will not betray their secret activities. An outbreak of paranoia would close that joint in a week."

"Good point. It wouldn't be a safe haven anymore."

"And our little argument was inspired," he went on. "It took him off guard, confused him. I think at the end there, though, he was a little tempted to hustle us off to a back room for a rougher interrogation. But people were watching us too closely by then."

"And would've wondered why he was mistreating customers."

Ryan slowly nodded with a reminiscent grin. "He had no choice but to push us on our way. And quickly."

"But he wanted to delay our return here, to give his goons time to turn this place over for the locket—"

"So he punctured my tire," Timothy finished. "Finding nothing, they went on to your condo." Maggie flinched as his breath fell across her ear. "I know this sort of danger is new to you, so I hope you'll be willing to do a little more listening from here on in."

She was instantly alert. "What are you trying to say, Ryan?"

"I think we should get the hell out of here, Maggie," he stated evenly, withdrawing his hands from under her jacket. "They may be on the way back, since I have no residence or office to trash."

Maggie opened her mouth, then shut it again. This poor man's private eye was smart. He knew how the bad guys operated. And he was right about her, too. She was tough, she was diligent, but she was inexperienced with the seamier side of the city.

Under all the muscle and unpressed clothes, Timothy Ryan was quite a guy, a man she could and would put her faith in. She rose swiftly from her chair and adjusted her jacket.

"What do you think we're dealing with?" she asked quietly.

His black brows arched in uncertainty. "Depends on Darla Faye, doesn't it? She's got Cramer on the ropes. His desperation is a wild card. We don't even understand it yet." With a firm hand on her elbow he steered her out to the reception area.

"We just have to find Darla for those answers."

"All in good time. We have to get out of here, Maggie. Now!"

"Stairs or elevator?"

"Good question. Let's opt for the elevator. It's quicker."

Maggie paused near the door with the strange sensation that she was forgetting something. "Stop. I have the feeling that Annabella needs something."

"I took the diaper bag to my folks—"

"She's grown quite fond of this small ratty blankie, I know," she said, pointing to a white crib blanket imprinted with faded teddy bears.

"Hey, that was mine," he retorted with a pained look. "It isn't ratty."

"Sorry," she said, suppressing a smile. She gathered it up and folded it in half. "Okay, I feel ready now."

Together they eased out the door, only to hear the hum of the elevator.

Her eyes grew wide. "It was a sign, Ryan. I know it."

"What?"

"The blankie! If I hadn't stopped for it, we'd have rung for the elevator by now and wouldn't have known anyone else was aboard."

He rolled his eyes. "All I know is that we need to be moving. C'mon!" He grasped her hand and led the way down the hall to the stairwell. They couldn't resist pausing by a huge potted palm, however, to see who emerged from the car. To their amazement, it was the bald maître d' and Adam Cramer himself! They stalked down the corridor and quickly ducked into her office.

"We've struck a huge nerve, haven't we?"

Maggie's stark whisper betrayed real fear, as did her trembling hand. He gave her fingers a comforting squeeze as he whispered in return, "C'mon, tiger. Your smallest client is counting on you."

Maggie beamed with gratitude. "When you're not saying the wrong thing, you're saying the right one."

Timothy knew the message itself didn't mean a damn thing, but the sentiment behind it spoke volumes.

"ONE HOUR the goons are looking for a locket, the next Adam Cramer himself is trespassing on my private property!"

Maggie mulled over the incredible turn of events a short time later at Ryan's Pizzeria, as she and Timothy sat together at the table reserved for family. They could've had their pick of seating, for the place was now closed for business, with the doors secured and red miniblinds shut flat against the front windows. Timothy's sisters and parents had already been introduced and were moving round the dining room, tidying up, closing things down. Sometime during the evening a portable crib had been delivered by Kate's husband, so Annabella was resting on a comfortable mattress beside them.

It was the kind of late-night coziness that the Ryans had always enjoyed. And Maggie had instantly felt welcome in an indescribable way that went beyond their acceptance of a new friend of Timothy's. It was as though she and Annabella belonged in the bigger picture, like the last piece of a family puzzle. It was crazy and frightening and wonderful all at the same time. Almost unbelievable to a woman who chose her acquaintances with slow, deliberate care.

Timothy was staring into the portable crib that flanked their table. Annabella, bundled up in a plush pink sleeper, looked like a porcelain dolly with an eiderdown body. The past half an hour had been wonderfully relaxing. He and Maggie had managed to calm down after their narrow escape back at the office. Timothy hated to return to the dirty business of Cramer.

"Maggie," he began, heaving a breath of reluctance, "I've been thinking about Cramer's personal appearance at the brownstone office."

Maggie set her hand on the sleeve of his suit jacket. "Me, too."

"Did you notice that unsightly bulge of his?"

"Yes, Timothy, I did," she sourly. "Unless he's seriously deformed, he was carrying a gun in a shoulder holster."

He grinned, admiring the comeback. "It's very important that we concentrate on the triangle of people involved in this case—Adam Cramer, Darla Faye, and Annabella. Figure out just how each one clicks into place."

"I've already thought the worst," she confessed, her loving green gaze following his to the crib. "Cramer's men may have alerted him to the playpen and the blankie. And he may be thinking that perhaps Darla had his baby on the sly."

"Yeah. Something only Darla can tell us for sure." He was relieved that she'd already digested the possibility on her own.

"It's understandable, I guess," she mused. "Darla wanting to keep her child free of that environment, that kind of father."

Timothy scratched his jaw in bewilderment. "It would be a mighty big secret to get away with though, wouldn't it?"

Maggie smiled wryly as she curled her fingers around her coffee mug. "Oh, I don't know. My mother thought I did it to her. Gave birth to Annabella, then hid her away."

Timothy's angled jaw slacked in surprise. "That must have been a shock, coming from your mother."

"It was more of a shock to learn that she hoped it was true!" she confided with a laugh. "Mother wasn't especially maternal while raising me. I couldn't believe she would want a grandchild."

"It seems our Annabella has the magic touch with everyone," he replied, smiling at his own mother as she bustled through the swinging kitchen door behind them with a carafe of coffee.

"Can I top you up, Maggie?" Kathleen Ryan offered, poised beside the table.

"Oh, no thanks, Mrs.—Kathleen," she corrected herself as she noticed the older woman's arched brow.

"Well, I think we'll be off, then," Kathleen announced, casting a look at her husband John who was lingering by the cash register. "The girls are gone and your father needs his sleep."

"Thanks for offering us the spare room for the night," Maggie said, reaching into the crib to stroke Annabella's head.

"As I said, it's not much," Kathleen reiterated apologetically. "An old couch, a double bed, a small bathroom. It's just right for us, when we've had a hectic night here and prefer to stay over."

"I know I can keep Annabella hidden here," Maggie said appreciatively.

"We all want you and the baby safe," Kathleen assured her. "Don't we, John?"

"Of course!" he bellowed across the dining room. "Just the idea of my son guarding the henhouse gives me a turn." His large features grew thoughtful. "Maybe we'd better take that little lass home with us."

"No, thank you," Timothy declined firmly. "We have our game plan and we want to stick to it."

"Doesn't take a rocket scientist to figure that everything you've told us so far about Maggie and Annabella is a pack of lies," John reproved him with the shake of a thick finger.

"Well, if you weren't such a nosy bunch, I'd more easily be an honest man," Timothy argued smoothly, privately irritated by the turn of events that had made this scene inescapable. How was he to know he'd be compelled to charge back here into hiding with Maggie? And all because Adam Cramer was not your ordinary club owner, but a tire-slashing, baby-chasing madman.

But, he thought wistfully, he had no call to be surprised by his parents' attitude. The price of sanctuary—or any other Ryan assistance, was always a soul-baring session just like this one. The expression No Questions Asked, was not one his mother would ever set to needlepoint, or his father would ever post on the dining room wall.

"So," John pressed, "do you plan to fill us in at all?"

"You know I can't discuss my cases with anyone, Pop."

"Can't tell the police maybe," Kathleen clucked in disappointment. "But your own family!"

Timothy pulled a hand through his black hair with a frustrated sigh. "Uncle Patrick is part of the family, and we want him and his badge to butt out right now."

"This has a lot to do with attorney-client privilege," Maggie inserted apologetically. "I think it's fair to tell you that Annabella is my client."

When his mother's round face remained set in a pout Timothy added, "How would you like the county taking care of the baby?"

Kathleen's mouth formed an indignant O. "Why, never!"

"All right then, Ma. If anybody asks for us, you don't know a thing."

John moved across the room with Kathleen's coat in his hands. "And we'll tell them you're a deadbeat who isn't welcome round here!"

Maggie's face crumpled in shock.

"He's teasin', Maggie," Timothy assured her, covering her hand on the Formica table. "Don't go overboard, Pop. Just a regular dose of the Ryan ignorance will do."

"We will manage," Kathleen answered, angling her arms into the black cloth coat John was holding open for her. "There is plenty of food in back for all of you. I took the liberty of sending Therese to the neighborhood market earlier on to get Annabella a little of everything."

Timothy stood up to kiss his mother on the cheek. "You're the best. Thanks."

"Get your own girl," John barked, with a wink to Maggie. "C'mon, Kath."

Maggie smiled as they walked arm in arm out the front door. Timothy trailed after them to resecure the deadbolt lock.

"They are wonderful," she said sincerely, bending over the crib to adjust the baby's covers.

"What about me, Maggie?" Timothy joined her at the crib as he asked the husky question. He reached out to rake back the curtain of hair tumbling into her face for a peek at her profile. "Well, then?"

She straightened up, her upturned nose wrinkled playfully. "Well, what?"

"Am I wonderful, too?"

"Perhaps. I'd go as far as to say we've reached a blind Billy between us."

He pinched her chin. "Ah, so you found out the meaning, my little know-it-all."

"Okay, so I only pretended to know and had to ask your mother," Maggie admitted. "But it fits us quite nicely. With care and patience, we should be able to stay on even ground, not overreach each other." With a sweet smile, she reached up to finger the collar of his beige cotton shirt.

"Seems only fair to tell you, then, that you're the woman of my dreams."

"O-o-oh . . . did you know you're intriguing, strong, pushy, sexy?" She moved her hands up around his neck and pressed her body into his solid length, intent on initiating a kiss.

"You're even pushier," he mumbled against her mouth. "But I love it."

"Anything else . . ." she coaxed with dancing eyes.

"Your hair is gloriously red, gold and orange," he murmured passionately. "Kissed by a fiery sea."

"Mmm, I think I'm going to love blarney," she purred, nuzzling into his throat.

"Oh, Maggie." He shuddered as he cuddled her close. "I think I'm going to love you for the longest time."

Maggie didn't protest as he began to peel off her suit jacket and tug the blouse from the waistband of her skirt. She was dizzy thinking about what he'd just said. This crazy man she'd known for twenty-four hours was professing his love for her! And he'd done it so easily, so convincingly—he'd simply stated the fact without analyzing it or testing it for loopholes and weaknesses.

His hands slipped beneath her blouse and skimmed over the silky fabric of her bra. Her nipples swiftly hardened to his touch, sending a sweet ache down through her body.

"What do you say we turn in for the night?" he suggested with short rapid breaths.

Maggie weighed the meaning of his words, flustered to distraction by his fingertips roaming her bare back.

It didn't take a detective to deduce that he wanted to share the only bed with her!

"Yes, let's," she replied in a hushed voice, her mouth curving in provocative invitation.

His features lit up another watt as he withdrew his hands from inside her shirt, smoothing it a little. "If we're careful, I think we can wheel this crib out of the dining room and into the spare room without disturbing the baby."

Maggie smiled down at Annabella, working her rosebud lips as though dreaming of a chocolate feast. "Let's give it a try."

The portable crib was old and creaky, but did roll easily. Within minutes they managed to guide it through the dining room exit and into the pitch-black room to the left of the kitchen.

"Hang on right here while I turn on a light," Timothy whispered, and moving through the dark with familiarity, he soon located a lamp near the bed.

With a hand still clutching the headboard of the crib, Maggie examined the small room, suddenly set aglow by a single bulb beneath a cracked yellow shade.

Never in her entire life had she slept in a room so stark. The walls were a pale green, the floor scuffed brown tile, and a square of navy cotton fabric, threaded through a narrow rod, served as a curtain for the only window. The mattress was miniscule compared to her queen-size one, with twin indentations, presumably made by the elder Ryans over the years. The orchid-figured bedspread was the economy type with a ruffle trim, a far cry from the rose satin ensemble complementing her carved walnut bedroom suite back at the condo.

But never in her entire life had she so looked forward to going to bed! Not in a chateau in the South of France, or a villa in Barcelona. She inhaled deeply, the anticipation swelling through her system, like a huge mounting wave.

Timothy, studying her from the old tweedy couch against the far wall, unconsciously unbuttoned his shirt and tugged it out of the waistband of his brown trousers. The verbal spitfire he knew was suddenly as silent as a lamb, looking over what was, no doubt, the most modest nest she'd ever seen. He flinched as he tried to visualize things through her eyes. She most likely was accustomed to lying on the finest linens, in the finest places. Of course, he consoled himself, doing it with Owen couldn't have been much of a thrill.

Still, a lesser man would indeed be a little apprehensive right now. As it was, he preferred to think his state of mind was simply confusion. Had she changed her mind about making love to him?

He cleared his throat, testing to see if he still had a voice, or if his throat was closed up tight. "Uh, Maggie . . ."

She started, her eyes widening. "Yes?"

"I, ah, hope you don't mind the place. Ma keeps it simple on purpose. The cooking odors seep into everything. They don't stay here much."

"Probably keeps it simple so you don't crash here too often," she teased, her green eyes sparkling.

"You do have the makings of a good private eye," he returned, his trepidation ebbing some. "If you'd like me to sleep here on the couch, I will."

It wasn't until that moment that Maggie realized that Timothy Ryan had an insecure bone in his body. Undoubtedly, there was only the one, but she found it very attractive indeed.

With a sultry look, she sauntered toward him. "You seem to have a strange preference for couches—the one back at the office, now the one here in the restaurant."

He cocked a brow. "Really? That's what you think is going on?"

She splayed her hands across his cotton shirt and pressed into the contours of his solid chest. "I think you're far too worried about the where, when you should be focused on the what."

His sighed resignedly. "You are used to the best, Maggie."

She gasped in dismay. "Since when don't you think you're the best, Timothy?"

A groan of amazement rose from somewhere deep in his chest. "You not only lust for me, but you know me." He cupped her face in his large hands and tipped it upward. The gesture sent her rich red mane tumbling down the center of her back. "I imagine all that hair tickles your spine when your skin is bare," he murmured, showering her face with slow, distinct kisses.

"Why don't we find out?" With a shrug and a rustle, she dropped her suit jacket to the floor. When her fingers stole to the buttons on her blouse, Timothy's hands were there to still them.

"I've been hoping to pop your buttons ever since our collision in the lobby," he purred in protest.

"We bumped into each other outside," she corrected.

"No—" He stopped himself. What difference did it make? "Either way, you're cutting into my territory."

Maggie released a shuddering sigh, her heart thumping in her chest as he fumbled with the small pearls on her crepe shirt. Fumbling was really the wrong word, she realized with a sharp intake of breath as the garment swished free from her body seconds later. "O-o-oh, Ryan!"

"Call me Timothy again," he coaxed, drawing her closer for a body-rubbing hug, and a mouth-searing kiss. "I love it when you do."

Sizzling sensations flowed over her, carrying her off into another world where only the touch of his mouth and fingers existed. She didn't even feel herself being stripped of her remaining clothes, until his hands were cupping the curve of her tight little bottom. With a cry of disbelief she stepped back.

"How..."

He gave her an uncertain smile. "How could I?"

"No, how did you?" she wondered incredulously. "I can't undress myself this fast!"

He wiggled his fingers with glittering eyes. "I can crack safes, pick locks, you name it. You name it, Maggie," he urged with an edge of seriousness.

She searched his features in the shadowed light and despite his proximity, he managed to avoid her gaze. She couldn't believe that this cocky, headstrong man was still unsure that she really wanted him!

She had to strip his clothes and his doubts away before she exploded! Balancing on one foot, then the other, she deftly stepped out of her hose and panties. Poised before him completely naked, she turned and strolled to the bed. She tossed the covers back, then turned to him with a provocative invitation. "Don't let me stop you . . . from breaking and entering."

"Spitfire move," he purred, with a dazed look. Even back in his imaginative, hormone-charged teenage years, when he'd crashed in this little room all by himself, he'd never managed to create the kind of alabaster goddess now standing beside the bed, inviting him closer! Her sleek, lean body gleamed in the lamplight—a creamy satin dream, with a russet dusting between her hipbones, topped with a rich tumble of hair that set her aflame like an erotic candle.

Maggie was as pliable as warm wax, and his pause to watch her from a distance with admiration and undisguised appetite, was heating the fire inside her to intolerable temperatures! Her body quaked as she lifted up her finger and crooked it in invitation. "Coming?"

The husky velvet voice promptly jarred him into action. He closed in on her with panther-like strides, and trapped her between his body and the mattress. Grasping her arms gently he squeezed them as though to make certain she was flesh and not just an apparition.

Maggie was very real indeed and her desires were urgent and earthy. With anxious, determined hands she worked with his belt and zipper, and delving into his briefs, stripped him clean.

"Love me." Maggie crooned into the shell of his ear. Standing on tiptoe to curl her arms around his neck, her solid nipples scraped into his crisp chest hair.

With a low growl, Timothy eased her onto the bed in the cradle of his muscled arms. The bed creaked and sagged as their bodies sank into the old mattress. Urging her flat on her back, Timothy captured one of her breasts in his hand, and toyed with its rosebud point before drawing it into his mouth.

Maggie lay with her legs splayed and her arms flung over her head, as she reveled in the sensations that spread from that single point of contact. She felt like a puppet on a string of fire, consumed by a burning spasm with every suckling pull. Timothy, delighted with his power, moved his mouth leisurely from one breast to the other, reached down to cup her intimate triangle in his huge roughened hand. His fingers squeezed her soft curls before plunging deep into her moist opening.

Maggie's soft cry of wonder was a foreign sound to her. And an aphrodisiac to Timothy, who raised up on his knees to trace his tongue down the center of her rib cage, dipped it into her navel with a flicking motion that sent a coil of heat through her belly.

He raised his head to hover over her with feasting eyes. Maggie trembled with anticipation as the seconds stretched out like years. Bending over her once more, he pried her thighs apart gently and invaded the soft skin of her inner legs with tiny kisses and nips. A wild fever galloped through her blood as he tasted her salty dampness, and expertly stirred her most sensitive points.

Maggie was nearly drowning in a vast sea of sensations by the time Timothy finally wedged his body over hers and seared his lips to hers.

Maggie dug her smooth, pointed fingernails hard into his back, then slid her hands down his spine. She arched her abdomen and, applying pressure to his buttocks, brought their lower bodies crushing together for a delicious melding. The pressure on his sensitive shaft sent a lightning bolt through Timothy's system. Rising up and rearing back, he thrust his hard length into her opening.

Together they gasped at the pleasure of the contact and lay quietly for a moment, sharing a hazy smile that affirmed their mutual trust and affection. Then Timothy moved again, and again, picking up rhythm and speed until Maggie surrendered to a climax with an ecstatic cry and Timothy followed with a shudder that made the mattress quake. They crumpled in a tangle of limbs and clung together, enjoying the closeness as their energies ebbed.

Timothy wasn't certain exactly when Maggie fell asleep, for he was lost in a fantasy of possessing her and a baby just like the one in the nearby crib. When her gentle little snore began to echo through the room, however, there was no doubt that she was completely out for the night. Careful not to disturb her too much, he aligned them both on the mattress until Maggie's head fit snugly in the hollow of his shoulder. Then he promptly fell asleep, and dreamt of his fantasy family with amazing clarity and yearning.

9

MAGGIE AWOKE Saturday morning to the sights and sounds of family intimacy. The curtain was pulled back from the window to allow in the bright sunshine. Timothy had scrounged up a fresh T-shirt and jeans and had positioned the baby snugly between them on the mattress, along with a large sturdy four-legged tray full of breakfast items, including orange juice, coffee, Danishes and fruit. Annabella, indescribably precious with her red curls tousled and a Raggedy Ann bib over her furry sleeper, was accepting spoonfuls of applesauce from Ryan.

"Yummy," he purred, his handsome face alight with mischief as he formed a circle with his lips. Annabella imitated his expression as she rolled the sauce around her mouth, and hit her palms on the tray with intermittent squeals, sending forth a fruity shower.

"Good morning," Maggie greeted them groggily, and inched back against the old maple headboard into a sitting position. She ruffled her tumble of hair, aware that Ryan and the baby were watching her. Suddenly self-conscious she gazed down to find her form clothed in the large white T-shirt.

"It's Dad's," Timothy said as her brow arched in speculation.

"He won't mind?"

"He'd want you covered." With a crooked grin, he steered Annabella's face back his way, urging another helping of fruit into her mouth.

Maggie sighed softly, caressing the baby's downy cheek. She felt a maternal lurch as Annabella's hazel eyes glittered at her with unconditional affection.

"I just can't believe what I've been missing...." she marveled.

"Thanks," Ryan replied huskily.

"I was talking about the baby," Maggie pointed out. "Okay, it would apply to us, as well," she added in response to his demanding frown. "Though that's the kind of remark the man is supposed to make, isn't it?"

"Well, consider it a mutual feeling," he answered with enthusiasm, dabbing Annabella's face with a damp washcloth.

Maggie chuckled, helping herself to some of the coffee from the insulated pot. "You really must've been a handful to raise," she murmured over the rim of her white ceramic mug.

"Yeah, I suppose," he admitted with a far-off look. "But I believe my folks had a good time bringing all of us up. It's never been dull," he conceded. "But it isn't supposed to be."

Maggie sipped some coffee and shrugged. "I think my parents were happy that I was rather dull as a child. Though, even if I'd had precocious tendencies, it would've been tough to be wild with my sixty-year-old nanny as my only companion."

"Ah, what a hell-raiser you would've been if you had a sibling or two," Timothy remarked.

She wrinkled her nose with delight. "Yes, I do think you're right."

"Three's a good number," he mused, nodding his dark head.

"Three what?"

"Three kids, of course!"

"Ah," she murmured, suffused with a warm tingle. "Guess I haven't thought much about that."

"I'm not surprised, with Owen in your be—life."

She glared at him over his near slip. "I think it's safe to say Owen is history, and not worth discussing."

"Agreed!" he said with undisguised delight. "I could go years and years without ever mentioning him again," he added in a significant tone.

Years and years? Her blue eyes gleamed in understanding. "I may just hold you to it, Ryan."

Timothy smiled broadly as he tipped a glass of orange juice against her mug in a toast. "Just hold me against you, and the rest will fall into place."

Maggie leaned forward to accept his kiss. As their lips met in front of Annabella, she clapped her hands together, then nuzzled their faces with her nose, in an effort to burrow into the action.

"This kid has your spunk," he murmured in wonder as they broke apart to include her.

"And your sense of humor," she retorted. "It's almost as though..."

"What, Maggie?"

Maggie laughed awkwardly. "Almost as though she is our very own!"

He pinched her chin in his hand, his expression sobering. "Careful now, sweetie..."

"I can't help becoming attached!" she cried back defensively.

"I know she's your first maternal experience, but you have to keep a little distance."

"Like you are!" she flared, hauling the baby into her lap.

His mouth twitched. "All right, so I'm nuts for her, too. But she doesn't belong to us. That's that."

"But maybe she might—"

"I very much doubt it," Timothy broke in adamantly. "I have the distinct feeling that Annabella has her own place, somewhere."

His fingers moved up to stroke her furrowed features. "If you want a babe, we'll just have to make our own. That's all there's to it."

"Oh, Timothy!" She sighed with loving exasperation.

"Anything to comfort you, Maggie," he answered with a twinkle. "I'm yours in every sense of the word. A baby-maker on call."

"The case is the most important thing right now," she forced herself to say. "As much as I'd like to hide out here with you forever, I guess that isn't very practical."

"No, honey, it isn't." He chuckled. "Sooner or later, my pop is going to need that undershirt back...."

With an obliging look, Maggie peeled off the shirt and hit him squarely in the face with it. Again the ivory goddess of last night, she slid off the bed to her feet, picked up the pieces of yesterday's gold and white ensemble, and began dressing swiftly.

Timothy averted his gaze to keep his desires in check. The case, the case, he would think about the case. "I suppose we'll have to stop tiptoeing around with Darla Faye and track her down for a face-to-face meeting," he suggested.

"Yes!" she agreed, wiggling into her pleated skirt. "So much centers around her relationship with Adam Cramer. We need some honest answers to defuse him! I don't mind avoiding my office for the weekend, but eventually I'll have other clients, other things to attend to. Including that tornado of a mess!" Her expression hardened. "Damn, I still can't believe that Cramer had the nerve to break into my office, and paw through my possessions!"

"The possessions were ours," Timothy swiftly corrected. "And my frustration matches yours. I'm not the type to back away from trouble, either. But we made the decision to accept Annabella as your client because of her dollar, and to keep her concealed so she wouldn't have to be given to the county."

"Would've been nice to have called the cops on Cramer and his pal," she declared wistfully, "and to have had them put behind bars for the night."

"Would've been nicer to punch him in the nose," Timothy muttered, a lethal glitter flickering in his eyes for the briefest moment. "But sometimes we have to yield," he added with a gentle gruffness, ruffling Annabella's soft curls with a loving hand.

There was probably nothing he wouldn't do for Annabella, Maggie realized, watching their interaction as he tipped the diaper bag's contents beside the baby seated on the bed. And she felt exactly the same way! Never before in her life had she hesitated to take whatever action she deemed fit. Last night, she'd turned tail and run, without a second thought. The move had been purely instinctive, with no thought to her files, her furniture—or anything else!

Maybe she wouldn't make a half-bad mother, given the chance.

"There are a lot of offensive moves we can make, without endangering the baby," she said, moving toward the bedroom doorway. "Starting with taking measures to have my office secured again. I know a good carpenter who can do the job, locks and all!"

Timothy, tussling with squealing Annabella's sleeper and diaper, directed Maggie to the telephone at the front of the pizzeria. Maggie flipped a couple of light switches to illuminate the shuttered dining room, then wended her way through the tables to the reservations podium in the alcove. She looked up the carpenter's number and wheedled him into putting her security job at the top of his list with a promise of double time. Then she punched a few more numbers to check her voice mail for messages.

The first one was from her mother. Helen wondered if Maggie still had the charming child, and if she'd like to bring her over to the Beacon Hill house for a visit. Maggie was sure her father hadn't told her about the condo incident of last night. They traveled the globe together like a couple of privileged vagabonds, but Sean O'Hara was an old-world protector through and through, who sheltered his wife from upsetting news whenever possible. Maggie believed it to be a mistake in general, but decided it worked to her advantage this time.

To Maggie's surprise, there was also a message from Emma Campbell, who left her home phone number and a frantic request to call. Maggie was sure Emma's call had to be connected to Darla—perhaps just the lead they desired right now. She quickly dialed the social worker.

Emma answered up on the first ring. "Oh, Maggie!" she exclaimed at the sound of her voice. "Thank goodness!"

Maggie braced her arms on the edges of the podium, excitement and hope lighting her delicate features. "Emma, tell me you've heard from Darla Faye again."

Emma inhaled with surprise. "You're right, she called again."

"I need to speak with her as soon as possible. What is happening with Darla?"

"I don't understand completely," Emma confessed. "Actually, I don't understand at all!"

"Emma," Maggie said urgently, "Ryan and I think we have a line on Darla and her troubles—"

"You must have stepped into the lion's cage because she's angry now, as well as frightened. Claims you've wrecked her life!"

Maggie clenched the receiver. "We're standing by, set to offer our total support."

"How nice of you, Maggie. I know this is charity to you—"

"Emma, has Darla spoken of contacting the police?" Maggie interrupted, thinking that if she reunited mother and child, the authorities could deal with Adam Cramer and whatever threat he was holding over the entertainer's head.

"No. When I first spoke with her she wanted to keep the law out of it, and she still wants no police."

Maggie sighed. She felt strongly that Darla should put Annabella's welfare above all else. But since Emma

Campbell knew nothing about the baby, she would have to save her arguments for the mother herself.

Maggie shifted from one foot to the other. "Did she tell you where she's staying, Emma?"

"Not exactly. She's not too keen on trusting you anymore," Emma lamented. "But of course I assured her that you are more than capable—if what she really needs is a lawyer!"

"She needs me, Emma," Maggie hastened to assure her. "Really, really, needs me."

"She insists you went too far—with whatever you did—and talked of skipping town...."

What on earth did the woman think she and Timothy would do with her baby, if she took off for good! "Emma, we must speak to her before she does anything so drastic."

Emma sighed into the line. "She did say that if you have something solid to offer her, she'll be at a roadhouse called the Yankee Rest in Concord this afternoon. It's out on Route 2A."

"Okay, we'll find it."

"I would very much like to come with you," Emma ventured anxiously. "Identify her for you, represent the county."

Just the kind of representation she didn't need! "No, Emma," Maggie cut in, a bit more sharply than she meant to. She and Emma had worked harmoniously together in the past, and would most likely do so again in the future, but this time the county's involvement would put Annabella at risk. "Darla is frightened enough as it is," she improvised. "Too many people might upset her. And we can identify her from the locket."

"Very well." Emma surrendered with a sigh. "Good luck. And please report back."

Maggie hung up with the promise that she would. She leaned thoughtfully against the podium for a moment, then she telephoned her mother.

Timothy was speaking to his own parents in the kitchen when Maggie burst in on them ten minutes later. Both the elder Ryans were dressed in casual slacks and shirts, ready to start preparations for the Saturday lunch crowd. Kathleen had her sturdy arms wound around the baby and was cuddling her to her chest. "Good morning, Maggie," the older woman said. "Did Timothy tell you this pink corduroy jumpsuit belonged to his goddaughter Colleen? Therese's child?"

"No, he didn't have a chance," Maggie admitted, stroking the baby's curved little back. "But it's lovely. Uh, Timothy," she ventured, keeping her voice light, "I have an appointment this afternoon. Thought you might want to come along."

"Sure, sure," he replied easily. "I suppose it would be easier to leave Annabella with my folks here."

"Oh, no!" The objection popped from her mouth, and all three Ryans stared at her questioningly. "It just so happens that I promised my mother that she could look out for the baby," she hastily explained. "I hope you don't mind."

"Sorry, Ma," Timothy said, grasping the baby under the armpits. "Guess it's Helen O'Hara's turn."

"Taking turns when it isn't even a relative?" Kathleen's lower lip protruded in disappointment. "Is she sure she wants to trouble herself with a strange baby?"

Maggie swallowed, privately thinking how strange the request itself was, considering that Helen O'Hara had never before showed much interest in a human being until he or she could appreciate an Impressionist painting. "Apparently she's fallen head over heels in love with Annabella, too!" she said with a laugh.

"Give us a flesh-and-blood Ryan to fall for," John Ryan blurted out, putting a beefy arm comfortingly over his wife's shoulders. "We'll share with these O'Haras."

"Pop!" Timothy chastised, as Maggie turned tomato-red.

"Of course you'll marry the girl first, boyo," John bellowed, not backing down an inch—like another Ryan Maggie knew.

"Things take time," Timothy pointed out with a glare.

"But nobody's getting any younger around here," John persisted. "And you two have that look, that look that Ma and I had. So get to it."

"I think we should get going," Timothy declared, looking around for the baby's red coat. A train of people followed him into the bedroom as he collected their belongings. "Dad, can we use your Jimmy?"

"What's wrong with your own car?"

Timothy and Maggie had left it at a service station a couple blocks away on Tileston Street the previous night, because Cramer could so easily identify it. "It wasn't running so hot, so I left it over at Wally's for a tune-up."

John lifted his shoulders and dug in his twill pants for his keys. "Oh. Okay. The truck's parked out back."

"If anybody asks, you haven't seen us," Timothy added, strapping Annabella into the car seat so they wouldn't have to linger in the lot.

"If your mother gets tired, we're a taxi ride away," Kathleen called to Maggie as they slipped out the back. "Tell her exactly where we are, won't you?"

FORTY-FIVE MINUTES later in her parents' lavish Beacon Hill home, Maggie gave Helen O'Hara precise directions to the pizzeria.

"Tired of Annabella?" Her mother's voice echoed sharply through the forest green and gray drawing room, her vivid blue eyes stormy as they followed her pacing daughter. "How could you even suggest such a thing, darling? How could you let her... Timothy, is it?"

Timothy, seated across from Helen and the baby in a velvet, deep-winged Federal period chair likely worth more than his car, smiled noncommittally at the elder O'Hara woman. Her chic cap of auburn hair, her large, pretentious gold jewelry, and her orange silk tunic certainly belied her Mother Earth sentiments. But the baby had keener senses than all of them, and she seemed content with her pink corduroy bottom planted in Helen's thin lap, fingering the glittering solitaire in her hostess's diamond engagement ring.

"Maggie has your comfort at heart first and foremost," he hastened to suggest with one of his infectious smiles.

Maggie watched Helen's instant delighted response. The O'Hara women were suckers for the Ryan touch. And to her own dismay, she had the feeling that seeing just how calculated Timothy's charms could be, wouldn't reduce their potency!

"Yes, Mother, I'm only thinking of you," she chimed in. "I know my drool and—all—used to make you edgy."

"Not all that edgy," Helen retorted, as she leaned forward to rub noses with Annabella.

"Never mind," Maggie said soothingly as the china mantel clock chimed the noon hour. It was the official beginning of the afternoon, meaning Darla should be at the Yankee Rest. "If you three will excuse me," she said hurriedly, "I think I'll just pop up to my old bedroom for a change of clothes."

Helen scanned yesterday's gold blazer and pleated skirt with a nod of approval. "Excellent idea, dear. You have a half dozen suits in your closet."

"How about something more casual?" Timothy suggested. "So we blend."

Maggie met his gaze and nodded. He meant that not only should they look like a credible couple, but perhaps like the kind of tourists who would stop to eat on Route 2A.

She reappeared in the drawing room ten minutes later in black jeans and a roomy, red, cable-knit sweater that would keep out the autumn chill. "We'll be back before dinner, Mother. Everything you should need for Annabella is in her bag," she said, gesturing to the quilted sack on the trestle table near the doorway.

"Please go!" Helen shooed. "Leave us to our fun."

"Including the phone number of the pizzeria," Maggie paused to add, rapping her knuckles on the table as she exited.

"YOU DON'T THINK you were a little too hard on Helen, do you, Maggie?" Timothy asked as he steered the Jimmy back down the O'Hara's winding driveway.

"Perhaps, but she is a babe herself about a lot of things," Maggie explained, staring out the passenger window at the lovely landscaped grounds, blanketed with a vast array of bright autumn leaves. "I mean, she's traveled the world without becoming worldly in a commonsense way. For instance, my father obviously didn't tell her of the trouble at my condo last night."

"Oh." Timothy arched a thoughtful brow. "To her credit, she seems quite bright, and current."

"Yes, of course!" Maggie instantly agreed. "She excels in her privileged niche. I'm not criticizing," she explained. "I was bound to follow in her footsteps, would have for certain, if I hadn't branched out and taken some chances."

"I'm thankful you did," he murmured, giving her one of his melting smiles. "It's the only way we ever would've connected."

They paused at the end of the driveway to wait for an employee back at the house to open the steel gate.

"One advantage this setup has over the pizzeria," Maggie observed as they rolled out into the street, "is the state-of-the-art security. If anyone dares enter the grounds without permission, all hell breaks loose!"

Timothy nodded, with a chuckle. "I'd say that the Ryans could raise a little hell for a good cause, but they couldn't compete with that."

THE DRIVE WEST of Boston to Concord was full of tense talk and creative speculation. Route 2A was a primary artery out of the city, but Timothy took a roundabout course through Cambridge and then Lexington, just to make certain they weren't being followed.

Maggie couldn't resist turning in her bucket seat at regular intervals to observe the traffic rolling along .

"All you're going to get is a kink in the neck," Timothy cautioned, his profile showing his amusement. "Let me handle the covert tactics."

"All right," she agreed, shifting back to face the windshield. "Guess I have enough on mind, trying to figure out how Darla could expect to skip town without Annabella. I can understand her being frightened of Adam Cramer for some reason, but why not make clear, concise arrangements for the baby? Surely she wouldn't expect me to bring Annabella to this roadhouse!"

"It's no place for our lass," he heartily agreed. "You'd think if Darla didn't want the baby any more, she'd have given her up to Emma Campbell," he mused. "No offense to you, Maggie, but she doesn't know you at all. It seems odd that she would entrust you with her child, even if you do have a reputation for being a hotshot attorney."

Maggie released a small sigh. "I know! But I am so flattered that she chose me. I guess it's a battle between common sense and a newfound maternal pride."

He gazed over at her for a brief measuring moment. "You wear it well, Maggie. Real well."

DESPITE ITS QUAINT Federal name, the Yankee Rest looked anything but cozy and inviting. It's rough timber shell, low slung design and gravel parking lot full of diesel trucks set it apart from Concord's historic clapboard buildings.

Maggie absorbed the sight as Timothy rolled into a parking space. "I was envisioning a mom-and-pop tourist trap," she confided.

"My guess is that Darla's no stranger to this place," Timothy said, killing the engine. "She probably feels safe here, surrounded by dependable muscle."

Maggie looked as though she had tasted something sour. "First the Colony Club. Now this."

"You'll get used to this kind of hangout," he assured her, patting her shoulder. "It's just new."

"So I should want to get used to it?" she demanded bluntly.

"If we're going to start blending some of our cases, which I have the sneaking suspicion we might," he speculated, "you won't be able to avoid places like this. Look at it this way," he said over her groan. "It will broaden your horizons."

He had a point. Ryan had been dropping many small hints about their linking up, in every sense of the word. And he had a way of making it all seem so natural. Maggie could find no quarrel with anything he was saying.

"Trust me, Maggie," he said, stroking her jawline. "There's no place I haven't been—now that I've been in your sinfully posh family estate."

With a steadying breath, Maggie entered the roadhouse a step ahead of Timothy, aware of the firm, supporting grip he had on her upper arm. The door slid shut behind them and they were suddenly sealed in a dark, smoky bubble. The only illumination was supplied by track lighting positioned along the low, peaked ceiling. The place had a timeless quality, where night passed into day and back without a sign. Presumably, a dandy place to hide.

"Keep moving," he directed against her ear. "She's probably tucked away someplace."

Fascination mingled with Maggie's apprehension as she made her way past a line of burly truckers shoveling up fried seafood from a steam table. The air smelled of cigarettes, sweat and fish and she raised a hand to smother a gag. She studied the faces as she moved forward, hoping for a glimpse of Darla among the patrons seated at the tables and in the wood-framed booths. To her amazement, everyone seemed jolly, content and comfortable among the World War I relics, and the stuffed bobcats and mooseheads mounted on the walls. She tried to loosen up herself, but found it impossible.

Maggie had begun to think that Darla had changed her mind again about their meeting when she noticed a woman seated all alone in a back booth.

"Darla!" Maggie disengaged herself from Timothy's grasp and eased into the bench opposite her without invitation. "I'm Maggie O'Hara," she added hastily, "and this is Timothy Ryan, a private detective I have on retainer."

In the dim light the entertainer squinted at her and Maggie had a moment to study Darla's face. Darla Faye appeared to be around thirty, as Maggie had guessed from her voice on the phone, and was quite pretty, with soft blond curls framing her smooth features. She was wearing no makeup, and she looked tired, vulnerable and frightened, despite her blazing eyes and mouth thinned in an angry line.

"You sound like the lawyer," Darla said finally. She picked up a cigarette and took a deep draw of smoke.

"Would you be speaking to me if you had any doubts?" Maggie asked.

Smoke poured from Darla's nostrils and curving mouth. "Sure, honey. You'd never make it back out the door in one piece if I cried out. If you don't mind, I'd like to see your identification. And have my locket back," she added, gesturing to the silver chain at Maggie's throat.

Maggie unclasped the locket from her neck, dropped it into Darla's palm, then dug into her purse for her wallet. She opened it up and showed Darla several pieces of identification boasting her picture.

"You too, Magnum P.I.," Darla directed with a toss of her blond head.

Timothy had always fancied himself a little more of a ragged Remington Steele, but didn't argue the point. "They don't deliver flat tires around here, for no reason at all, do they?" he asked dryly, flashing his license.

"Yeah, I heard you were over to Adam's place," Darla shot back.

"We're assuming you left the napkin as well as the locket," Maggie pointed out reasonably. "Surely you were trying to lead us to the Colony Club."

"I was," she granted. "I wanted you to scare the hell out of Adam Cramer for me."

"Now, how did you expect me to do that, Darla?"

"Well, I would've told you, if you'd been in your office for our appointment," Darla answered accusingly. "Gotten this thing done right!"

Maggie tossed her flaming hair back and squared her shoulders. "I *was* there! Except for a few minutes. I saw someone fleeing on the stairs and assumed it was you. Naturally, I took up the chase!"

"Well, I showed up, and your place was empty, with the lights on.... It was like you had vanished. I got spooked and ran."

"Why are you frightened?" Timothy broke in to ask. "Why are you hiding?"

"As you found out at the Colony, I was an entertainer there, in the lounge. And Adam Cramer's girl for quite some time, too."

"Adam Cramer's a married man, isn't he?" Maggie prompted, recalling the man's reference to his happily married state.

Darla shrugged, her air indifferent. "I thought he was going to leave his wife for me. Desperately wanted him to, until I inadvertently found out he was in deep with the syndicate. Entertaining all those two-faced creeps at his place didn't bother me at all. But holding hands with the mob . . . Hell, I just wanted out."

"Nothing has ever been proven against him," Timothy pointed out. "Cramer's always managed to cover his tracks."

"Until me, until now," Darla announced bitterly, stubbing out her cigarette. "I lingered at the Club after closing one night, going over some new numbers, rearranging the lighting and sound. I was crouched behind an amplifier, when Adam and three other men came in and seated themselves at the bar. I knew Adam would be furious to find me there so I decided to stay concealed, and ended up witnessing a high-level meeting that I wasn't supposed to."

"What's he up to?" Maggie prodded.

Darla took a long draw from a glass of whiskey. "Adam's gotten in on a drug shipment that will involve players in Colombia and Miami. These wise guys want to use the Colony Club for their distribution point."

"Well, somehow he found out you found out," Timothy surmised.

Darla nodded forcefully. "Almost made it out of there, but he must've spotted me out in the parking lot through a window. Came charging up on me." Darla took a shaky breath, obviously reliving the encounter. "I truly think I'd be dead, if I hadn't been lucky enough to be halfway into the driver's seat of my Honda. We had words, with my car door between us. He made some threats, I made some promises." Her expression grew wan. "He didn't buy my loyalty claim. Slapped me hard across the face. Called me a useless bitch, among other things. I realized then that all his pillow talk had been lies, that he'd never looked at me as more than a toy."

"How did you get away?" Timothy asked quietly.

"Socked him right in the kisser!" she declared triumphantly with a closed fist. "He only staggered back a little, but it was enough to give me clearance to get inside my car, lock the doors, and speed away. I'm sure he tried to follow, but he had to get his car out of the underground garage first. I had enough of a head start to get clear."

Darla sighed, and sagged tiredly. "I've been in hiding ever since. Of course I knew I couldn't do that forever, so I decided to contact somebody who would steer me toward a decent female lawyer who could nose around Adam Cramer's place and give him the signal that I could be trouble if he gave me any trouble."

Maggie absorbed the details, and drew some obvious conclusions. "So you wanted to use me to let him know that someone inside the establishment knew about you and your position."

"Yes, a kind of insurance. Letting him know you had the locket that could be traced back to him, and that you might have my statement in writing, seemed like enough to keep him at bay."

"Yes, he wanted that locket!" Timothy inserted. "Probably anxious to collect whatever we had that was yours."

He hazarded a glance to Maggie, who was following his train of thought. *Anxious to collect the baby, too.*

"In theory, I believe that your plan might have kept him clear of you," Timothy said. "Wouldn't have stopped the drug deal, though."

"Hey, that's not my problem," Darla snapped defensively. "I only want to be left alone."

"But you've always had a duty to report his activities to the authorities!" Maggie cut in. "Stopping a shipment of drugs this big is a huge moral duty."

Darla put another cigarette into her mouth and flicked it to life with her lighter. "I'm sorry, Maggie, but my own skin is all I care about."

Timothy and Maggie shared another significant look. Poor Annabella.

"Well, all of this has gone completely haywire," Timothy growled.

"Yeah," Darla agreed. "The word is that Adam's stepped up his search for me since you were at the Club, is determined to find me no matter what. It was supposed to work the opposite way, people," she scolded. "Instead of taming him down, you've got him revved up! Just how did you manage to do that?"

So this is what Darla meant when she told Emma Campbell that they'd ruined her life. Maggie cleared her throat, and leaned over the table. "We're quite certain he wants the baby, Darla, at least as much as he'd like to keep you silent about the drug deal. Doesn't he have children of his own?"

"Baby?" the singer repeated blankly.

"Yes!" Maggie hissed.

"He doesn't have children of his own. Said his wife couldn't manage it." She rolled her hard brown eyes. "But he never suggested I give him a child."

"Now, Darla," Maggie ventured, flexing her fingers as she summoned up patience, "we don't have time for games, either. Isn't Annabella Adam Cramer's child?"

"Annabella?" Darla was quite clearly perplexed.

"The baby in the basket," Timothy prodded.

"The baby in your office?" Darla asked, openly nonplussed.

"Yes!" the pair impatiently chorused.

"Just what did you propose I do with her, Darla?" Maggie sputtered. "You must've had a plan!"

Darla rapped the table angrily. "That kid was there when I got there," she told Maggie. "I assumed she was yours, so I just stuffed the napkin and locket in her basket so you wouldn't miss them."

The sound that bubbled from Maggie's throat was somewhere between a whimper and whine. She felt Timothy's large hand close over hers on the table. "Our dear, sweet Annabella is a whole different client entirely," she squeaked.

"Apparently so," he muttered in wonder.

Darla's gaze shifted from one to the other. "You thought the kid was mine? All this time?"

"It stood to reason, Darla," Maggie snapped. "I left my office for a matter of minutes, and when I returned the basket, with your locket in it, had popped up out of nowhere! And you left a one-dollar retainer."

"That doesn't matter now," Timothy cut in. "We have to move forward, find out who Annabella belongs to, and convince Adam Cramer that he isn't a father after all."

"So that's why he's suddenly absolutely insane!" Darla exclaimed furiously. "He now has another reason to eliminate me. To get the child for himself!"

"Darla, it would be so helpful if you gave him a call," Maggie urged. "Explain that the baby isn't yours."

"I don't want to get involved!" Darla insisted, taking another gulp of whiskey. "And I never hired you, anyway—that wasn't my dollar!"

"Please give it a try," Timothy begged. "You must've had some good times, some level of faith in each other. Just give it to him straight and hang up. It might just be enough to slow him down."

"I'll think about it, okay?" Darla promised. "But he's going to be awfully busy tonight with that drug deal of his. I didn't catch the place, but I did catch the time and the date, and today's the day!"

10

"IT'S LIKE ANNABELLA popped up out of nowhere!" Maggie stared blankly out the passenger window of the Jimmy as they sped along the freeway back to Boston. Both of them felt an indescribable urgency to reunite with the baby. "Her parents are floating around out there somewhere...." She trailed off in frustration. "Why use me? Where are they?"

"It's a crazy twist of events, finding out that we have two separate cases on our hands," Timothy conceded with a grimace. "And now we've got a pressing problem concerning her information about Adam Cramer's drug deal."

"I know Darla and I don't share the attorney-client bond of confidentiality!" she said, wringing her hands in her lap. "And I concede that we have an obligation to report Cramer's criminal activity. I can't wait to nail that bastard! But we can't let Annabella get caught in the crossfire. I would never forgive myself."

Timothy's fingers tightened on the steering wheel as he made a sharp lane change in order to keep up his speed. "If only Adam Cramer hadn't realized we were holding a baby, and mistaken it for his. We could've tipped the cops on his deal and stepped back. Now he will hound us relentlessly in his search for the truth about the baby."

"If only Annabella's real guardian would show up. We could hand her over and Cramer's claim would stop right there."

"We can't count on a miracle like that, Maggie."

"I know. I'll just have to make my own miracle. I'm determined to keep that baby, Ryan, until a very responsible guardian appears, with a very plausible explanation!"

MAGGIE BROKE into a run as she and Timothy entered her parents' home shortly after three-thirty. "Mother! Where are you? Mother!" She paced on the marble floor of the huge open-ceilinged foyer, waiting for Helen O'Hara to appear. "She couldn't be far, Ryan. With the baby and all . . ."

Moments later, Helen floated down the curving walnut staircase in a flowing white damask robe, a black sleeping mask raised up to her auburn hairline. "Calm yourself, darling. I was just about to take a nap."

"Is Annabella napping?" Timothy asked, venturing toward the staircase.

"Why, no," Helen lilted, moving to join them. "The funniest thing happened while you were away—"

Maggie grasped her mother's arms. "Where is the baby, Mom?"

"Why, the father came for her!" Helen exclaimed in a bell-like voice. "Diaper bag and all."

Maggie turned to meet Timothy's horrified gaze.

"We had the loveliest visit, he and I. Talked all about his wife and you. Why didn't you tell me she'd married a dashing continental?"

"Who, Mother!"

"Your old school friend, of course. Amanda Springer, the tennis champ."

"What's she talking about, Maggie?" Timothy thundered, as angry as she'd ever seen him. They already both knew who the dashing continental was!

"I told my mother that Annabella belonged to an old classmate of mine," Maggie swiftly replied.

"Doesn't she?" Helen asked in confusion.

"No, Mother, we don't know who she belongs to," Maggie explained. "She's a client of mine. I was trying to keep her situation a secret in order to keep her safe."

"Fine job we've done!" Timothy threw his arms up in the air.

"I thought the security here would suffice," Maggie said apologetically.

"He was too smart to use brute force," Timothy answered. "He rolled right through all the state-of-the-art gadgetry with an old-fashioned dose of phony charm."

"Didn't the baby cry out in fear when he took her?" Maggie asked.

"Why, no, she was sleeping at the time," Helen replied.

"If only she'd awakened," Maggie lamented. "She would've screamed to high heaven. I know it!"

"How could this John Smythe have not been the father?" Helen queried, pressing her hands against her hollow cheeks.

"John Smith?" Maggie repeated incredulously. "You fell for that, Mother?"

"Pronounced mundanely its sounds common and fake," her mother granted, averting her gaze. But he spelled his name S-m-y-t-h-e, and pronounced it with a long *i* sound. And he knew all about everything," she added defensively. "He even knew the Provence hideaway that Sean and I frequent in the summer. Knew the farms and the shops."

"He fooled you with geography and flattery, then," Maggie admonished. "Got you sidetracked enough to ramble on about me and Amanda Springer!"

"Well, you should've told me the score from the start," Helen retorted indignantly, pulling her robe tighter around her miniscule middle.

"But nobody around here ever tells you anything unpleasant," Maggie shot back.

Helen gasped in affront. "And that's my fault, too?"

In a big sense it was, Maggie thought to herself. Helen liked her sheltered existence very much. at least she never expressed any complaints. "Look, Mother," she murmured. "I'm sorry I have to be so blunt. But the clock is ticking. We must recapture Annabella."

Helen's bright blue eyes were filled with concern. "What does this John Smythe want with her?"

"His name is Adam Cramer, and he's under the misapprehension that Annabella is his daughter."

Helen fingered the mask atop her head. "Well then, he certainly won't harm her, will he?"

Maggie threw her hands in the air. "I don't know! He must want a child very badly."

"Well, this isn't my fault," Helen staunchly maintained. "Truly, it isn't."

"No, Mother," Maggie acknowledged with a heaving breath that racked her entire body. "This is my responsibility entirely. I blew it."

MAGGIE AND TIMOTHY returned to the office to plot their next course of action. Thanks to Adam Cramer,

Maggie literally had to wade through Timothy's belongings to get to her desk. Assuming Cramer's residence was unlisted, she went straight to her computer and an information network shared by the city's attorneys. She quickly hit the jackpot with his Cambridge address, in a posh neighborhood overlooking the Charles River. It seemed like the logical place for him to take Annabella.

Maggie jotted down the address on her scratch pad, then came to the realization that Timothy hadn't followed her in from the reception area. "Ryan! C'mere, quick!"

Timothy loomed hesitantly in the doorway. "Maggie, I—"

"I have Cramer's home pinned down."

"That's fine, honey," he said quietly.

She looked up at his strong immobile form. "We really have to get the hell over there right now! Show a little energy, will you?"

"I called my Uncle Patrick," he informed her evenly.

"Already! Without asking me? Really, Ryan!"

"He's on his way over, Maggie. Just the mention of Adam Cramer and drugs in the same breath got him going. He promised to arrange a posse if we have something solid."

"I know Cramer has to be stopped," Maggie said furiously, "but couldn't we have made a move for Annabella first?"

"And risk her well-being again?" Timothy challenged quietly. "Honey, that guy has to live in a fortress and I don't even own a peashooter, much less a gun. He'll also be expecting us, so we wouldn't even have the element of surprise."

"Maybe he'll expect us to give up," she proposed, "let his guard down because he believes he has a right to the child."

"He also could drop us with a shot to the temple, then claim we were burglars caught in the act." Timothy hated being so blunt, and he hated watching her face crumple. "I am as much to blame as you are for allowing this situation to get out of control. That's why it's so important that we play it by the book from here on in."

Maggie leaped out of her chair, fists clenched, primed for a fight. Timothy cupped her cheeks in his hands and stroked her cheekbones with his thumbs as tears sprang to her eyes.

"But I just feel like she's all mine, Ryan!"

"I know, I know," he crooned. "But this is the only way. Good investigators—and lawyers—know when they're cornered. We need the help of the police for this showdown, that's a simple fact."

They were sharing a comforting embrace when Patrick Ryan called out from the reception area. He quickly appeared in the inner office, dressed in a pale blue cardigan and gray corduroy trousers beneath his dark topcoat.

It was the first time Maggie had ever seen the large, white-haired man out of uniform. But somehow, with his intense look and alert eyes, he seemed on duty even now. And the gun in his shoulder holster backed up the impression.

"Uncle Pat!" Timothy greeted him, enveloping him in a huge hug. Maggie, leaning against the edge of her desk during the exchange, observed that they were identical in build and similarly featured. "Hope we didn't wreck your Saturday," she murmured politely.

"Not if you've got something on that slime Cramer, you haven't," he rumbled. "Tell me everything, you two," he directed. "And I mean everything."

Together they related their story, from their first meeting until the moment they discovered Annabella missing from Helen O'Hara's home.

Patrick paced the room, rubbing the back of his thick neck. "This is outrageous even for you, Timmy. And Maggie..." He clucked in disapproval. "It's not like you to skirt laws as you have with this baby."

"I assure you it was all above reproach," she insisted with a toss of her flaming head. "Annabella is my client, and will continue to be after she is returned to us."

"That's debatable."

"Be happy we've included you now!" she cried out angrily. "I was all for storming Cramer's house myself!"

Patrick reared in shock. "And Timmy was the voice of reason?"

"This once," Timothy confessed, shoving his hands into the pockets of his jeans. "Look, according to Darla, Cramer's got that drug deal going down tonight someplace. Between that and the kidnapping, the police should be able to tie him up for awhile!"

"It would be mighty nice to speak to Darla Faye," Patrick mused with a creased forehead. "Make sure the facts are clear."

"Let me try her at the Yankee Rest," Maggie hurriedly suggested. She rolled her chair up to the desk and went about getting the number from information, then dialed the roadhouse.

"She doesn't want to be involved," Timothy cautioned. "That's the reason she contacted Maggie rather than the cops."

"She's scared," Maggie added, pressing the receiver against her ear as it rang on the other end. "We did try to appeal to her conscience, though. We asked her to call Cramer with the news that the baby isn't his."

"Great idea, before he took the child," Patrick retorted.

"Surely he won't harm Annabella when he learns the truth!" Maggie fretted.

"If an ego like that believes he's sired a child, it'll take a lot to convince him otherwise," Patrick pointed out on a consoling note. "He'd demand tests, and those would require time. And that's all we need, a little time."

Maggie managed to coax Darla Faye to the telephone, then rose and waved Patrick into her chair. He sank down, took the receiver, and began to speak to Darla in a tone as warm and fluid as Irish whiskey, presumably draining her dry of information at the speed he was taking notes.

"There now, miss," he said soothingly, sounding much like his nephew. "We plan to catch him red handed, so you won't be called in to testify at all. Yes, it's the baby that will do it for us. Oh, you did?" Patrick's ruddy face narrowed. "Well, I appreciate your honesty. Yes, I understand that she did. Goodbye."

"What was she saying, there at the end?" Maggie demanded anxiously, leaning over him and squeezing his burly shoulder. "The part that you didn't write down."

Patrick met her gaze squarely as he weighed his answer. "First off, Darla believes the child is at Cramer's

Cambridge home. It's secure, relatively secluded, his refuge." He heaved a heavy sigh as Maggie's manicured nails dug deeper into his muscle. "She said that at your urging, Maggie, she called the Cramer house and left the message that the baby is not hers, and therefore not his."

"Oh, no!" Maggie squealed. "But I directed her to do that before we knew the baby was taken! I didn't mean—"

"I understand," he assured her smoothly.

"Well, who did she speak to at the Cramers'?" she pressed.

"You've got to be strong, Maggie," Patrick advised. "Darla spoke to his wife."

"So she's there, too?" Maggie queried bleakly. "With Annabella?"

Patrick nodded his gray head soberly. "Darla heard a babe's cry."

"Dammit!" Timothy thundered. "We've got to get the hell over there, Patrick!"

"Isn't the kidnapping charge enough, Patrick?" Maggie chimed in.

"We shall make our move," the older man promised. He picked up the phone again and Maggie and Timothy listened mutely while he arranged for a warrant to cover all the circumstances. "I'm afraid that a good attorney could get him a simple slap on the wrist for taking the baby by pleading him temporarily off his rocker or something," he explained as he hung up. He rose to his feet. "But a cocaine deal should pull the plug on Cramer for a good long time."

"We've got to get over there before he leaves for the meet," Timothy urged.

Patrick nodded. "If we're lucky, we may just find some incriminating evidence in that house of his. Amazingly," he marveled, "this break is due to that dear little lass. She's giving us access to a criminal we thought untouchable." As he herded them out the door he added, "Yes, kids, I'd say that baby Annabella is heaven-sent."

11

"SO THERE YOU ARE, Adam."

Adam Cramer stood in the foyer of his Tudor mansion and watched his wife descend the carved wooden staircase with the baby in her arms.

Twenty years ago he'd have been delighted to see Althea on those same stairs with their child. But they had remained childless as the years had passed. And in Adam's mind, the passage of time had transformed Althea from a cool blonde who'd turned his head with every move, into a cold silver-haired bitch who turned his stomach with every word.

He'd decided, after this Colombian cocaine deal went through, he was giving up the club, giving up their life completely. He was going to take his child to Europe, perhaps Italy and raise her there.

Such dreams drew a smile to his face as he hung his coat in the small closet near the door.

"We need to talk about this child," Althea announced, her almond eyes snapping.

"I directed you to watch over her," he responded briskly. "Even you should be able to handle such a simple task."

Althea stepped onto the tile floor and circled him like a menacing tigress. "Again, I am asking where this girl came from, Adam."

His mouth thinned dangerously. "And again, I am telling you it is none of your damn business, woman. I have an important meeting scheduled for tonight, and I don't have time to play games with you. You've been instructed to care for the baby and that is what you'll do!"

"For a close friend, you said?" she questioned tartly.

"Yes," he hissed, making Annabella's cherub face pucker in fear. "Are you deaf as well as dumb?"

"You've gone too far this time, Adam," she sneered in return. She gasped as Annabella threw her curly red head back and begin to wail. Althea quickly set the baby on the floor and watched her silently crawl away. The child was nothing more than a nuisance. Not to mention heavy!

Adam ran his long fingers through his hair, and stalked off to the study on the right. He switched on the overhead light, drew the heavy brocade curtains over the windows facing the street, and made a beeline for his wall safe, hidden behind an original watercolor by John James Audubon. He decided he would take the picture with him. After all, an old Colony Club patron had gone to a lot of trouble to steal it for him. Both his house and the club were full of such items acquired by light-fingered club members. It would undoubtedly be difficult to choose in the end. He hauled a briefcase out of the safe, and set it on his desk. He clicked it open to reveal stacks of bonds.

"Negotiable?" Althea asked with interest.

Adam extracted a sheet of paper from the inside pocket of his suit jacket, and scanned it. "Perhaps," he returned breezily. "But nothing for you to worry about."

Althea moved closer and saw that the paper was a hand-drawn map of Boston's Inner Harbor area. "It appears you have a payoff arranged."

He shrugged fluidly. "Maybe."

She folded her arms across her narrow chest. "Have you purchased us a baby? On the black market perhaps?"

"I have bought you nothing," he assured her.

"I certainly hope not! The idea of buying a child doesn't interest me in the least!"

"You know I have no interest in anyone else's children, Althea," he returned curtly, snapping the leather case shut again. "I was planning to tell you under calmer circumstances, but you see, the little girl is mine. I sired her."

Althea's harsh laughter contained a dash of genuine amusement.

He gave her a lethal look. "I tell you, the girl is mine."

"I very much doubt it," she said with a laugh. "You are sterile."

Adam raised his manicured hand, and slapped her soundly across the face. Althea stumbled, but stood her ground. "You are defective, wife," he said harshly. "That is why we have no children! A woman who is a hundred times the female you are has provided me an heir. I will not let you spoil it!"

"Darla Faye? A hundred times more woman?" Althea's features brightened despite the ugly red splotch across her cheek.

"What do you know about Darla?" he asked coldly.

"I've known for months that you and that tacky singer are lovers," she admitted. "What you don't know is that she called here just today, to assure you that she is not the mother of this baby girl you've stolen." She shook her head. "This is a new low, even for you, Adam. You've taken somebody else's baby. So desperate for a child, you've woven some tale—" She broke off with a scream as he grabbed a handful of her silver-streaked hair, and drew her ear to his mouth.

"Listen to me, you idiot. Neither you nor Darla will stand in my way. The baby has to be mine. That is all. Now collect her things. I am taking her to my meeting."

Althea nodded, eager to get out of harm's way. "Everything's on the bench in the foyer."

Adam strolled out of the room after her, calling out to Annabella in a strained voice. "Baby? Where are you, little one? Come out of hiding."

Althea paused near the mirrored parson's bench, fingering the handle of the diaper bag. "The kid doesn't know what you're talking about. And she's too young to hide!"

"If I can't find her, I'll make it difficult for you," he vowed nastily, before moving into the living room at the opposite end of the foyer. "As it is, we are through. If you want to salvage your life, you'll shut up and obey."

"Through?" she seethed in disbelief. "Just like that? Over this child?"

A security phone connected to the guardhouse fronting the estate began to buzz back in his office. "Get in there and answer that!" he thundered. "No one is to be admitted," he directed as she scurried by him. "No one."

"Baby... Baby..." he called as he peered behind a burgundy-colored wing chair. He turned toward the arched entrance as Althea came back into view. "Well?"

"It was a club patron, James Henderson," she claimed airily. "I advised the guard to give him the usual brush-off."

"Just a minute..." Adam stalked back into the foyer just in time to see Althea open the front door. A barrage of uniformed and plainclothes policemen flooded inside. He remembered belatedly that Henderson had dropped dead of a heart attack a week ago.

"After twenty-five years," he raged, making an attempt to lunge at her, only to be stopped by two officers. "How could you, Althea?"

"After twenty-five years, there's only one way you're going to leave me," she snarled back. "And that's for a trip down the river!" She raised her thin arms in the air with a grand sweep. "Let me show you where the bonds are, gentlemen! And there's a handy little map to get you where you're going!"

Maggie rushed forward, her tearstained face as pale as a sheet. "The baby," she demanded hoarsely. "Where is she?"

Althea turned to her with a tiny smile. "I really can't say. She had the good sense to evade my husband and I haven't seen her since."

Maggie and Timothy exchanged frantic looks.

"She's down on the floor someplace," Althea added genially. "Now who is in charge here? Let me show you to the study...."

"Annabella!" Maggie screamed at the top of her lungs. "Where are you, honey?"

Within seconds the baby's little red head popped into view from behind a huge potted plant in the corner of the foyer. "Cho-cho!" she squeaked, her hazel eyes wide.

"Thank heavens!" Maggie pressed her fingers to her mouth and swallowed a sob of relief.

Timothy charged ahead and scooped her up in his arms. Annabella clung to his neck with a chubby arm lock and a whimper.

"I told you she knew what she was doing," Maggie said, falling against Timothy's chest to hug them both.

"Good thing somebody does," Timothy retorted, kissing each flaming redhead with sound smacks. "Now let's get out of here," he suggested. "These nice policemen have work to do."

"Timmy, lad!"

Timothy released a frustrated breath as Patrick detained them near the door. "Yeah?"

"Just want to help you through the police tangle outside," his uncle announced jovially.

"That's great, Uncle Patrick!" Timothy said gratefully.

"It's on the condition that bright and early Monday mornin', we get together to discuss what's best for this little lady," his uncle said, giving Annabella's head a pat. "That is, if she isn't claimed tomorrow."

"Tomorrow?" Timothy parroted.

"I have put a large notice in the Sunday *Beacon*, asking for any information on our orphaned friend."

"It's a deal," Maggie surrendered. It was a lot better than losing her to the authorities tonight, she realized.

"C'mon, Maggie," Timothy coaxed, putting a comforting arm around her shoulders. "We'll just have to make the best of the time we have left."

Maggie took her makeshift family back to her condo that night. Annabella fell into a deep, exhausted sleep, and Timothy helped Maggie break in her queen-size mattress. Even though it was a couple of years old, it was plain to see that it had never really rocked before....

SUNDAY MORNING CAME all too soon. The trio assembled in Maggie's office to await the outcome of Patrick's notice in the newspaper. With so much nervous energy to displace, Maggie had donned purple tights and a leotard under her white knee-length sweater with the intention of doing a little tap dancing.

Timothy winced when she dug into her bottom desk drawer for her tap shoes. He couldn't help but remember all the thumps he'd endured during his time in the office below. "Must you, Maggie? Today of all days? When we have so much on our minds?"

"It'll be just the distraction we need." Maggie sat down on the hardwood floor and eased her feet into the black buckled shoes. She smiled endearingly up at the denim-clad man seated on the leather chair near the window with the baby on his lap. Annabella was dressed in her original outfit, just in case her parent's turned up. "I'm sure you'll enjoy the show more in person than you did from below, Ryan." With a coy smile she rose and pulled off her sweater to reveal her skin-tight ensemble.

Timothy released a low whistle. "Hey, maybe you've got a point."

"Switch on the music, please," she instructed with a gesture toward the cassette player on the desk.

"When you're right, you're right," he enthused moments later, ogling her luscious legs as she clattered in time to the music.

Annabella squealed nonstop, as Timothy clapped her hands gently inside his own.

When the music died down, Maggie was breathing in short, satisfied gasps. "Bring her over here, Ryan."

His black brow arched and his clear blue eyes darkened in suspicion. "Why? We'd rather just watch."

"Since when!" Maggie puckered her lips and crooked her finger. "I'm going to show you there's more than one way to rock."

The next song began several seconds later. Before long Maggie had Timothy and the baby moving their feet to the beat, with her hands wedged under Annabella's armpits for support. They didn't hear their visitors enter from the hallway, didn't notice them until they were standing in the door to the inner office.

The dancing threesome froze in their tracks at the sight of the youngish couple with the elderly lady between them. Timothy rushed over to the player and shut off the music.

"There she is!" The auburn-haired woman rushed forward and scooped Annabella into her arms. "Annabella, sweetie! You gave mommy such a scare."

"Your grandmother gave us the scare," the man corrected dourly. Extending his hand to Timothy, he said "We're the Cranes. I'm Neal and this is my wife, Joan, and her grandmother, Annabella."

Maggie watched the reunion dumbstruck. As new as the picture was, it was remarkably right. Annabella was purring like a kitten in the woman's arms.

Timothy struggled with his frozen jaw to form a cordial smile, then introduced himself and Maggie. He reminded himself that this was what they wanted—for Annabella to have her family back! But he understood the anguish in Maggie's green eyes and shared it to the bottom of his heart.

"Another Annabella," Maggie finally managed to murmur.

"Yes, the baby is Grandma's namesake," Joan explained with a toss of her bright red curls. Joan's resemblance to the child cuddling in her arms was uncanny. "We can hardly believe what's happened ourselves, much less explain it to you."

"Please try," Maggie urged, folding her arms across her chest. She had no intention of releasing the baby unless she was completely satisfied with their story.

"Grandma dropped her off here by mistake," Neal announced, his temper strained. "She thought this was my brother-in-law's office. He is a chiropractor in a brownstone up the street. Anyway, we've been out of town, and thought that the Annabellas were together all the while."

"Grandmother had a blackout last Wednesday night, lost her short-term memory," Joan added in explanation. "In any case, we just got back in town late last night. And all hell broke loose when Annabella's story appeared in the paper this morning. We rushed down to the police station and they sent us over here."

"Oh." Maggie swallowed hard.

"I am so sorry, all of you," the old woman murmured, seeming contrite, and a little disoriented even now.

"We know you are," Joan said consolingly. "It was more than you could handle. And no harm's done, dear."

"What about the note, and the dollar?" Maggie asked.

"I wrote the note to my son, from the baby," the elder Annabella explained. "I always gave him dollar bills as a boy, for doing me favors."

Maggie cast a look at Ryan. They sure had a lot of inside information.

"Patrick Ryan is parked down in the loading zone, taking a call on the radio," Neal explained. "He came along to back us up, to assure you that our story is real."

"We appreciate how well you've cared for Annabella," Joan hastily assured them, squeezing the baby tightly against the folds of her mauve coat. "Officer Ryan told us how diligent you've been in keeping our baby safe and sound."

"It's been an adventure," Maggie said in a choked voice. She turned her welling eyes to the doorway as Patrick entered.

"So I see things have been straightened out," the large patrolman bellowed genially.

"Hello, Uncle Pat," Timothy said with a wry look. "You didn't have to worry, we haven't been giving them the third degree."

"You'd never do such a thing to the lass's folks," Patrick replied confidently. "And they are the right ones, Maggie," he added gently. "Guaranteed by the Boston Police Department."

"Well, I guess there's nothing left to say," Maggie announced with a sniff. She moved toward the room's small closet and produced the wicker basket Annabella had arrived in. Her blanket and bonnet were still inside. "It's hard to imagine this frail Annabella carting around the baby in this basket," she mused aloud.

"And she must be mighty quick on her feet, as well, to have escaped detection during the whole episode," Timothy added, stroking his square chin.

The old woman exchanged a look with Joan and Neal, then turned to smile at Maggie and Timothy. She seemed to radiate a remarkably comforting light. When she spoke, there was nothing feeble about her delivery. "Sometimes, children," she said with a small sigh, "we just must have unquestioning faith in ourselves and each other. Can you understand?"

"Yes, I believe that's a lesson we've just learned," Maggie breathed in reply, basking in unmistakable solace. Suddenly, remarkably, everything seemed all right—things were as they should be for Timothy and herself and Annabella.

"Time for us to go now, Annabella," the old woman murmured, grasping the wicker basket with her veined hands.

Annabella raised her head from Joan's shoulder, and twisted to face Maggie and Timothy. Her huge hazel eyes were rich with love and devotion. "Cho-cho?" she gurgled.

"No chocolate," Joan said firmly.

"Cho-cho!" Annabella screamed desperately.

"I have a little chocolate here, I believe." Maggie rounded her desk and opened her pencil drawer. Sure enough she found a stray truffle, wrapped in silver paper, nestled between an eraser and a ballpoint. "If it's all right with you . . ." she trailed off hesitantly.

Joan nodded. With shaky fingers Maggie unwrapped the mound of soft candy and pressed a little into the baby's small pink mouth. She burst into tears when Annabella placed her pudgy hand on her cheek and gave her a wet, chocolaty kiss.

"Take your time, folks," Patrick invited as he left. "I'll be down in the squad car, ready to take you wherever you want to go."

Timothy moved closer to kiss the baby's temple. "Bye-bye, baby," he cooed, as he watched Annabella curl her fingers around the truffle in Maggie's hand. She had managed to enclose it inside her soft little fist by the time the adults started into the reception area.

Maggie tried to follow in her clacking tap shoes, but Timothy held her back with a firm grip around her waist.

"Goodbye, goodbye," Maggie called out to the closing door.

"Hello, hello," Timothy corrected, turning Maggie against him. Pushing her hair over her shoulders, he clasped her face and showered it with tiny kisses. "It's the way things are supposed to be," he whispered. "And only the beginning for you and me."

Maggie melted into his comforting warmth. They had been kissing for some time when the outer door popped opened again. Still locked in an embrace, they turned to find Patrick standing before them with a bewildered expression.

"So where are they?" he boomed impatiently.

"We don't know," Timothy replied, cuddling Maggie closer. "They would've hit the street a long time ago."

"But they didn't!" Patrick objected, his large features flushed with frustration. "I couldn't have missed them coming out. I swear!"

Timothy and Maggie groaned in unison. "Not this again!"

"I tell you, they disappeared!"

"They have a right," Timothy insisted firmly.

"Not on my beat, boyo!"

Maggie gave him a radiant smile. "This is where we came in on this case, and this is where we're going out. See ya around, Uncle Patrick."

Muttering to himself, the tired old policeman stomped out the door.

Timothy looked down at Maggie with twinkling eyes. "He really liked it when you called him Uncle."

"You think so?" she asked hopefully.

"Yeah . . . Or will, when he gets over his huff."

Maggie fingered the collar of his denim shirt. "Think your family will be happy to hear you proposed to me last night?"

"I think they already take our marriage for granted."

"And children?"

"Yes, please," he growled longingly, tugging her closer. "One wedding and one baby, coming right up."

"Think we can make a baby as precious as Annabella?" she wondered, her delicate features creased in worry.

"All I can say, Maggie," he purred with dancing blue eyes, "is that we'll give it our very, very best shot."

Epilogue

Six years later

"MARY MARGARET RYAN! Get out of that tree!"

A perky five-year-old with a crown of fire-red curls peeped out from the juncture of a U-shaped oak tree in the middle of the Boston Common. "Yes, Mama."

Maggie, who was seated on a park bench watching the other children's game of tag on the bright green grass, was certain that the sweet, perfunctory reply was little more than a brush-off. She shook her head and warned "Not an inch higher, you hear!"

"No, Mama."

Maggie gave the baby boy in the old Ryan family buggy beside her a pat. "Your sister is a fiesty one, Mikey, boy. Remember that a little caution goes a long way in this world!" The raven-haired child smiled sweetly up at her before he drifted off to sleep.

Maggie tipped her head back a fraction, closed her eyes, and luxuriated in the feel of the fresh June breeze on her face. She sensed a familiar presence behind her, but pretended not to.

"What a lovely creature," a husky masculine voice purred in her ear.

"Ah, but I am a married woman," she protested. "Oh, but perhaps . . ."

"Maggie!" Timothy exclaimed in mock dismay as he rounded the bench. "You in the habit of flirting in the park?"

"With our three children and a parcel of their cousins?" she asked incredulously. "Who'd dare approach me?"

He chuckled deeply, and reached in the buggy to ruffle his younger son's hair. "Guess there's lots of advantages to this family style of living." He turned to the huge oak where the young crowd was whooping it up. "Do you think our daughter should be in a tree?"

"No, Timothy, I don't," she answered emphatically. "But she is bullheaded like her mother," she added as he dipped down to kiss the tip of her freckled nose.

"And compassionate like her too," Timothy said. "And indispensable with her brothers."

"So much love to give," Maggie sighed. "On her own terms always."

Timothy cupped his hands around his mouth and shouted with authority. "Mary Margaret, get out of the tree!"

"Yes, Daddy!"

"That should do it." Timothy eased onto the bench, eyeing the handled basket between them. "When are you going to spread out the picnic? I'm starved!"

Maggie shrugged. "I've been holding off because of the clouds."

Timothy picked through the basket and snagged a pickle with his fingers. He munched on it with a carefree grin, glowing with boyish delight. "Isn't this just perfect, honey?"

"Yes," she murmured, reaching over to finger the lapel of his navy suit. "The way we've made our dreams come true with our three perfect children. On days like this, when my mind is free and clear, I think of our meeting, our plans—"

"And you think of Annabella," he finished knowingly.

"Yes," she affirmed with a wry look. "You know me inside out, don't you?"

"Guess we're just a match made in heaven."

"I still wonder if she's all right," Maggie said with a sigh. "I think about that frequently, because Mary Margaret reminds me so much of Annabella."

"Biting into chocolate, or pursing her lips into a pretty pink rosebud," he offered in example.

"Which is just what we ordered, as I recall," she said dreamily.

To their delight the sky suddenly opened up overhead, sending a brilliant ray of light down on the park.

"Time to spread out the eats!" Timothy rejoiced, rubbing his hands together.

"I have the feeling that she's all right, don't you?"

"Well, sure," Timothy replied. With his hands clasped behind his head he gazed at the frolicking children. "Though I must say, Patrick will never get over losing track of those people that last day."

Holding hands over the basket, they shared an intimate laugh.

"Tim Junior needs a haircut," Timothy observed, eyeing their elder son's strawberry-blond mop as he scurried around the oak after his cousin. "Take him over to his Grandma Kathleen's for a summer buzz."

Maggie's creamy forehead furrowed. "His Grandma Helen has fits when I do. Thinks it's high time the children went to her salon."

"No child of mine is going near a scissor-toting neurotic named Montrose!"

"Kathleen it is," she promptly surrendered.

Timothy chuckled deeply. "No argument, Maggie? Just for the exercise?"

She offered him a flirty wink. "Maybe I prefer to save my energies today. For tonight . . ."

"Spitfire move . . ." He beamed his approval. "As it happens, we're going to be spending some time together this afternoon, too."

"But the children—"

"I've already put my mother on standby," he broke in to explain.

"What do you have up your sleeve, Ryan?" she demanded silkily.

"Shop stuff, I'm afraid. I dug up some real facts on the Burns lawsuit. It's urgent that we have a meeting with your client before court tomorrow."

"You are such a taskmaster!" She pursed her lips in a pout. "I liked you better as a lazy private eye who tempted me into playing hooky half the time."

He turned to her, concern in his blue eyes. "I've got too many mouths to feed to act like that now—"

"Hey, hey, look at me," a high voice chirped triumphantly.

Maggie and Timothy turned toward the oak tree. Mary Margaret had scaled the other side of the tree and was balanced precariously on a branch near the top.

"No, darling, no," Maggie whispered, biting on her fist.

"Not a word, Maggie," Timothy cautioned quietly. "Get up and move very carefully."

They were halfway across the grass when a piercing scream split the air, and they saw her small body, dressed in her red-and-blue jumpsuit tumbling through the green leafy branches. Maggie did scream then. At the top of her lungs, with her eyes scrunched shut.

When she opened them, however, Mary Margaret was rounding the tree safe and sound, charging at Timothy who was now several steps in front of Maggie.

"Mary!" Maggie raced forward to join father and daughter, and enveloped them in her arms. Warmth surrounded them, filled them, calmed them.

"Remember this same feeling, Timothy?" she said with a sniff. "Remember?"

The day in Maggie's office when they had to give up Annabella. "How could I not remember," he whispered, gazing down at the child who could pass for the other baby any day of the week.

With Mary Margaret braced between them, babbling that she was just fine, they staggered back to the bench. Maggie and Timothy sank down on the wooden slats and looked at their daughter with stern, teary eyes.

"You were naughty to climb after we said no," Maggie chided.

Mary rocked on her heels, her hazel eyes downcast. "Sorry, Mama."

"How did you manage to land unharmed?" Timothy's feelings were a blend of relief and disbelief.

"A little girl helped me," she replied simply. "She was very, very pretty."

Maggie scanned the distance looking for a stranger. "I'd like to thank her."

"She's too shy to come over."

Timothy wondered how much his creative child was embellishing the real story. "Are you sure you didn't land on some leaves?"

"She lifted me up in her arms and carried me to the ground!" Mary Margaret blurted out, then waited with wide hazel eyes for the dramatic effect the announcement would have on her parents. She was disappointed when, instead of objecting loudly, they absorbed the news in silence. "Can I go play now?"

"Yes, shoo," Timothy said, giving her a gentle shove. "But you stay off that tree. And I mean it!"

"Okay, Daddy!" Mary stomped her foot with her hands on her hips.

"Tell the children we're going to eat in a few minutes," Maggie added.

Mary ducked into the buggy and gave her little brother a kiss on the head before darting off.

"I'm still shaking," Maggie confided to Timothy as they unfolded their large plaid picnic blanket on the grass beside the bench.

"I'm feeling pretty shaky, too," he said, showing her his own trembling hand.

"Timothy, you don't think that Annabella... I mean the way she appeared and disappeared so strangely..."

"I don't know," Timothy answered honestly. "Sometimes . . . I just don't know."

Once the bowls and sandwiches were in place, they called all six children to lunch. Maggie made sure everyone got a full plate, and Timothy, cradling baby

Mike for a bottle feeding, got comfortable against the bench.

The moment Maggie mentioned dessert, she felt a charge like an electric shock down the length of her spine. She rose on her knees, reached into the basket, and removed a three-layer chocolate-fudge cake. "Look at this, children!" she cried. "I made it just for you!" Her announcement brought shouts of glee from the children. Maggie held the cake overhead, enjoying the moment, basking in the sunshine and the laughter surrounding her.

"Mama! Mama!" Mary said in hushed wonder, tugging at the jacket of Maggie's green nylon sweatsuit. "Here she comes."

Maggie's head turned automatically toward the big oak tree. Skipping across the grass was a young redhead, a bit older and lankier than Mary Margaret, dressed in a flowing white dress. "Timothy! Look, darling, look!"

His features softened in awe. "It can't be her, Maggie," he cautioned. "Don't get your hopes..."

The pair froze in wonder as the girl neared them, her hazel eyes aglow, her rich red hair a curly curtain fanning her shoulders.

It was Annabella, a seven-year-old Annabella.

Maggie wanted to touch her so badly. But she found she was completely paralyzed! Trapped in a moment of time, watching... feeling... enjoying...

Annabella reached out to Maggie and stroked her temple with gentle fingers. Maggie smiled with enchantment, then frowned in shock when Annabella drove her fingers into the chocolate cake, took a huge handful of the fudgy confection, and pressed it into her mouth. A second later she was standing before Timothy and baby Mike. She ruffled Timothy's hair with her clean hand, leaned over to kiss the baby on the same spot Mary had only moments ago, and then she was gone.

Timothy started, and moved slowly like a man waking from a deep sleep. It had seemed like a brief, vivid dream, but no, Mike had a huge chocolate spot on his tiny forehead. He turned to Maggie, who stood stock-still, holding the damaged cake, looking as if she hadn't breathed since Annabella had touched her.

"You okay, honey?"

Maggie turned to him, her face gleaming with pleasure and satisfaction. "I've never felt better, Ryan. As of this moment, my life is complete."

MOVE OVER, MELROSE PLACE

Come live and love in L.A. with the tenants of Bachelor Arms. Enjoy a year's worth of wonderful love stories and meet colorful neighbors you'll bump into again and again.

From Judith Arnold, bestselling author of over thirty-five novels, comes the conclusion to the legend of Bachelor Arms. Whenever a resident sees "the lady in the mirror," his or her life is changed and no one's more so than Clint McCreary's. Or Hope Henley, who looks exactly like the mysterious woman. Don't miss Judith Arnold's captivating:

#561 THE LADY IN THE MIRROR (November 1995)

#565 TIMELESS LOVE (December 1995)

Believe the legend...

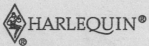

HARLEQUIN®

Don't miss these Harlequin favorites by some of our most distinguished authors!
And now you can receive a discount by ordering two or more titles!

HT#25593	WHAT MIGHT HAVE BEEN by Glenda Sanders	$2.99 U.S. ☐ /$3.50 CAN. ☐	
HP#11713	AN UNSUITABLE WIFE by Lindsay Armstrong	$2.99 U.S. ☐ /$3.50 CAN. ☐	
HR#03356	BACHELOR'S FAMILY by Jessica Steele	$2.99 U.S.☐ /$3.50 CAN. ☐	
HS#70494	THE BIG SECRET by Janice Kaiser	$3.39	☐
HI#22196	CHILD'S PLAY by Bethany Campbell	$2.89	☐
HAR#16553	THE MARRYING TYPE by Judith Arnold	$3.50 U.S. ☐ /$3.99 CAN. ☐	
HH#28044	THE TEMPTING OF JULIA by Maura Seger	$3.99 U.S ☐ /$4.50 CAN. ☐	

(limited quantities available on certain titles)

AMOUNT	$
DEDUCT: 10% DISCOUNT FOR 2+ BOOKS	$
POSTAGE & HANDLING	$
($1.00 for one book, 50¢ for each additional)	
APPLICABLE TAXES*	$_____
TOTAL PAYABLE	$_____

(check or money order—please do not send cash)

To order, complete this form and send it, along with a check or money order for the total above, payable to Harlequin Books, to: **In the U.S.:** 3010 Walden Avenue, P.O. Box 9047, Buffalo, NY 14269-9047; **In Canada:** P.O. Box 613, Fort Erie, Ontario, L2A 5X3.

Name: _____

Address:_____ City: _____

State/Prov.: _____ Zip/Postal Code: _____

*New York residents remit applicable sales taxes.
Canadian residents remit applicable GST and provincial taxes.

HBACK-OD2

URBAN COWBOYS

A Stetson and spurs don't make a man a cowboy.

Being a real cowboy means being able to tough it out on the ranch and on the range. Three Manhattan city slickers with something to prove meet that challenge...and succeed.

But are they man enough to handle the three wild western women who lasso their hearts?

Bestselling author Vicki Lewis Thompson will take you on the most exciting trail ride of your life with her fabulous new trilogy—**Urban Cowboys.**

THE TRAILBLAZER #555 (September 1995)

THE DRIFTER #559 (October 1995)

THE LAWMAN #563 (November 1995)

HARLEQUIN® Temptation®

HARLEQUIN®

Temptation®

Secret Fantasies

Do you have a secret fantasy?

Holly Morris does. All she'd ever wanted was to live happily ever after with the man she loved. But a tragic accident shattered that dream. Or had it? Craig Ford strongly reminds her of her former lover. He has the same expressions, the same gestures…and the same memories. Is he her fantasy come to life? Find out in #566, LOOK INTO MY EYES by Glenda Sanders, available in December 1995.

Everybody has a secret fantasy. And you'll find them all in Temptation's exciting yearlong miniseries, **Secret Fantasies**. Throughout 1995, one book each month focuses on the hero and heroine's innermost romantic desires.…

SF-12

HARLEQUIN®

CHRISTMAS ROGUES

is giving you everything you want on your Christmas list this year:

- ☑ -great romance stories
- ☑ -award-winning authors
- ☑ -a FREE gift promotion
- ☑ -an abundance of Christmas cheer

This November, not only can you join ANITA MILLS, PATRICIA POTTER and MIRANDA JARRETT for exciting, heartwarming Christmas stories about roguish men and the women who tame them—but you can also receive a FREE gold-tone necklace. (Details inside all copies of Christmas Rogues.)

CHRISTMAS ROGUES—romance reading at its best—only from HARLEQUIN BOOKS!

Available in November wherever Harlequin books are sold.

HARLEQUIN  PRESENTS®

Don't be late for the wedding!

Be sure to make a date in your diary for the happy event—
the sixth in our tantalizing new selection of stories...

Wedlocked!

Bonded in matrimony, torn by desire...

Coming next month:

THE YULETIDE BRIDE by Mary Lyons
(Harlequin Presents #1781)

From the celebrated author of *Dark and Dangerous*

A Christmas wedding should be the most romantic of
occasions. But when Max asked Amber to be his
Yuletide Bride, romance was the last thing on his mind....
Because all Max really wanted was his daughter, and he
knew that marrying Amber was the only way he'd get
close to their child!

Available in December, wherever Harlequin books are sold.